Train Diaries

ELDRED ROGERS

Order this book online at www.trafford.com/06-2097
or email orders@trafford.com

Most Trafford titles are also available at major online book retailers.

Note for Librarians: A cataloguing record for this book is available from Library and Archives Canada at www.collectionscanada.ca/amicus/index-e.html

ISBN: 978-1-4251-0340-8

We at Trafford believe that it is the responsibility of us all, as both individuals and corporations, to make choices that are environmentally and socially sound. You, in turn, are supporting this responsible conduct each time you purchase a Trafford book, or make use of our publishing services. To find out how you are helping, please visit www.trafford.com/responsiblepublishing.html

Our mission is to efficiently provide the world's finest, most comprehensive book publishing service, enabling every author to experience success. To find out how to publish your book, your way, and have it available worldwide, visit us online at www.trafford.com/10510

www.trafford.com

North America & international
toll-free: 1 888 232 4444 (USA & Canada)
phone: 250 383 6864 ♦ fax: 250 383 6804 ♦ email: info@trafford.com

The United Kingdom & Europe
phone: +44 (0)1865 722 113 ♦ local rate: 0845 230 9601
facsimile: +44 (0)1865 722 868 ♦ email: info.uk@trafford.com

10 9 8 7 6 5 4

Train Diaries

Slight Stutter!

My name is Ellis and I have been regenerated!

Hmmm, opening gambit done and dusted!

Train Diaries indeed, I hear you say. Yes another diary has made it through the layered cells of the subconscious. Shredding the fragments of reality and imagination with the bold but slightly whimperish scream of read me, read me, read me.....!

I feel that the whole business of diaries should be confined to the pages it's written on and certainly no further than the four walls of the originators room. I mean who wants to enter your deepest, pleasant, dark, neurotic and sometimes insane thoughts? But sometimes, just sometimes, it is in these nether regions that beauty is conceived and if allowed, springs forth to enlighten and question mind-sets. So this diary is definitely an exception to the rule.

As with everything, when you get past the stage of self criticism of; 'will they like it or not', then the whole story and purpose begin to emerge. As you read these encounters, especially one with a guy called Idika. I hope it will affect you and you'll see why and understand the particular person and reason that led me to write the Train Diaries. It changed my life and made an indelible impression on my spirit, soul and body.

Ah, now you're getting the insights into why this diary can't be suppressed. Read – enjoy and let it sink in.

Enough already, I am reading it so get on with it, I hear you say!

Morning Cheer!

Just like most people in London, I commute to work using South West trains. Unlike some, I haven't been forced onto public transport by 'red' Ken's congestion charge. In fact, I have something in common with the mayor, despite now working outside the charging zone. I have always been an advocate and user of public transport. Not because I'm in favour of any green issue, far from it, and neither am I opposed to any green issues. Just had to mention that also, since these guys are militant and I don't want them camping outside my yard.

I commute for the simple reason that it allows me to read books, cuts out the hassle of shouting, tutting or outswerving other motorist. And ah! The other commuters, now they make every train journey eventful and enjoyable. Public transport definitely gets a hoot from me. What a total mixed blessing!

Nothing beats those nameless faces that are unconsciously weaved into your life without prior consent. If you ask me, in a society where everything is geared towards privacy and isolation, these encounters hold tiny shreds of links to a community or rather a sense of community. The fragmentation of this essential part of man's existence is such, that even daily occurrences of encounters such as saying good morning on this mutual journey to work, disorientates a few. In major instances a full scale nervous breakdown might be on the cards.

Try it one day? Say good morning to a stranger on your route and see how it pierces through the exterior and ignites an internal combustion so strong that every ounce of blood will be drained off their face and used to put out the impending fire your words just lit. If the response of good morning too, is late in coming, it is because of the shock factor involved. Trust me, the impact carries a Richter scale of about 5 and if said with a smile – boy it's off the charts.

The mind can't find a reason quickly enough to justify why a stranger would say good morning to you with a smile. Reasons that follow go in two directions. The first focuses on why the person will do such a thing. And the second is fully based on causation – what did I do to invite this response.

The first set would consist of reasons such as: strange person, Oh how nice. What a happy friendly human being. Are they on drugs? Maybe they're lonely and trying to make friends. Perhaps I know them from somewhere. Etc

The second set of reasons would be: They sense I'm nice and successful. They admire me. My friendly aura lured them in. Perhaps I know them from somewhere. I look like I need cheering up. Maybe they think I'm lonely.

I have deliberately omitted a crucial reason. That's if it's directed at the opposite sex, you know the first one you get fed by your depraved mind would be; they fancy me!

Quite funny but even mundane reasons of familiarity of travelling together each day is just too simplistic for the mind.

Greeting people you encounter most mornings should be practised by all. And when it's said, don't just say it for the sake of it with a toothless grin for a smile. Let those pearly whites glow. Or rather let those coffee and cigarette stained dentition help you spread some morning cheer. Oh and say it from the heart.

A fear that most people contend with and so avoid such niceties is that people might go beyond good morning and start asking how you are and next thing you know, they might want to make friends – dread horror, just sends cold shivers down the spine – psycho alert!

Okay that's the morning psychological analysis covered!

Back and Forth!

These people that I've encountered and encounter every-day on my journey can be classed as extras in a movie, with no lines of course, except when I decide to accord them a line.

In this sense you might get carried away and think you control your daily occurrences, but I strongly believe in divine influence, altering things periodically. Sort of, God letting you know that He is in charge. And since I subscribe to Shakespeare's observation of the whole world being a stage, the unseen director contradicts (good or bad) or changes the script without consent. Allowing these people to speak, react or act obnoxiously or pleasantly. But the difference is if you know the Most High intimately, it will always be in your favour.

This aspect although on a smaller scale is the fun part of commuting in particular and existence in general. They create and constitute background noise from time to time. Predictability is certainly not for the living, so thank God it happens.

I don't want my every day journey laced with people standing or seating with books and newspapers covering their tiresome, sleep weary faces. I understand covering those stress lines and sleep weary faces but don't do it for fear of exposing your dull, insular, mundane and predictable lives. Interaction is necessary and a little encounter with the next human might just change your life and give you that impetus you need on this long road – called life.

If you're like me and find meanings in things, the lesson from this opening salvo is: chat and open up just a little to the next commuter – but follow your heart.

I mean these people, these commuters!

These smartly dressed hardworking people. Now I use the term hardworking loosely – there's just no point in emphasising what hard work consist of.

Back to my mini rant!

These shabbily dressed people with their riotous colours and clothing. What am I talking about! The only colour shades you'll find are on the adverts that adorn the billboards splashed all over the station. (By station I'm referring to Clapham Junction, as Mitcham Junction and Syon Lane are not advertising hot spots). Not even the sky can compete with the persistent colour scheme of the great British public. I mean talk about chalk and cheese. If it is not black, navy blue or brown it certainly won't fly. Dark colours, okay! And thank you very much – we are British and we like 'daw'! Oh, and woe betide you if you happen to wear a light shade of cashmere brown, you'll stick out like a sore thumb – you flash git – what are you trying to prove – what? That you have flair, I mean we probably earn more than you!

These people that sip their lattes and cappuccinos with their smug look because they are desperately trying to buy into and depict the fad of; professional, laptop bag carrying, palm top using, ipod listening (with its conspicuous white ear phones) and mobile phone chattering urbanite.

These pre-pubescent people that scream and fill the station with chattering of their school gossip, latest crush and spontaneous A capella song renditions that would make the contestants on X-Factor sound like Black Mambazo. Maybe, they've heard that Tracy Chapman, Rod Stewart and Shola Ama (the last two only added for reference purposes and it ends there) got spotted singing at train stations. Word of advice, pack it in, all the A&Rs watch talent shows and take their cue from Simon Cowell. They have a preference for singers (voices) that can be repackaged 'no frills' style to cover old songs and that's the established norm. You get me!

These people that bop around the platforms arms wide open, with paint (dirt) stained jeans, caterpillar boots or white addidas trainers, fleece tops, track suit bottoms and sometimes tool boxes. These ones that walk around the platform, chest sticking out with a look that cries; I am a real man. I work outdoors with my hands in the cold weather and I don't get flu. I lift things, drive monster vehicles and wear a helmet. I don't sit around all day poncing in front of a computer surfing the net. You won't see me ordering a sandwich with fancy Italian names. Ooooh, excuse me, 'can I have a panini with green pepper fillings and a sprinkle of parmesan – oh and don't forget the mocha – get off! I'll tell you what a real man's sandwich is, chips and bacon butty drenched in huge dollops of ketchup and brown sauce – now that's lunch'.

These chain smoking people, you fill the air with the putrid and rancid smell of those cancer sticks. Bellows of smoke that refuse to rise upwards, instead it clings to my soft cotton gear that was immersed in Fabreeze with a little squirt of Cool Waters for that extra allure or in Thierry Henry's words; "that certain je ne sais quoi". You stump the butt on the floor, then expose your tar stained teeth in defiance. Not pretty........but I don't think your disposition even allows you to contemplate the pitfalls of smoking.

These people that put my nostrils and stomach under pressure every morning from the smell of their Chanel no5 perfumes, CK BE aftershaves and body odours. Oh, let's not mention your farts, civilised eh! The unwritten train etiquette dictates that you hold it in, until you get off, so it can be 'gone with the wind'. And this is coming from a guy that brews and savours the effervescence of his farts.

You shove and push once the train arrives, jostling for position with little shuffles of your feet, doing your best ostrich impressions to spot the spaces between Clark's finest and the train door. You think your actions go unnoticed. I mean your ability to inflate and deflate your weight to edge your self forward and get that seat your monthly Travelcard warrants is downright impressive.

A mention has to go to those mini races that take place in the tunnel between platforms. Trying to out-walk your fellow commuters under the guise of hurrying for the train – yeah right! You know how long it takes between platforms – grown up children. Its fun though, isn't it? Especially when you out-walk everyone that got off your train.

These people that steal platform standing spots, train seats and window view. These Metro reading public that also feel they have the right to read yours! Oo! Get yours before you get on the train or wait until I am done.

These people that offer a refreshing smile, sometimes. Although I feel, it happens when they haven't seen me or that particular person in a while. Maybe the smile is a huge relief on their part, since it restores the normality of their commuting existence. It must quell any suspicion that I had escaped the route. Or a promotion at work has upgraded and catapulted me into the company car status, because driving to work becomes mandatory (congestion charge or not).

The departure of one commuter from a prescribed route causes a slight but deep uncertainty in the mind. Due to this, others might be forced to re-evaluate the route, leading to job changes or changes in train times. I mean we don't want you changing your route it gives us ideas that you're moving up the ladder. We don't want to be reminded of our routine - working for the man. The smile though, is only for that day....phew! We thought he left – ah, everything is back to normal.

These people! The ones that see the station and journey as a way to ensnare a mate – get a life. It's too early in the morning and in the evenings folks just want to get home. Frankly your lust and boldness is quite appalling and lacks any sensitivity to your fellow commuters. We don't possess that kind of audacity or ease in which you strike up a conversation with under tones of a lurid act to follow. Word of advise, speed dating cannot be practised on the platform either. The waiting time borders on seconds, heavily bearing on the efficiency of the service of course. So cut it out, we are seriously trying to digest the daily news served by those 'desk journalists' at Metro and fine job you do too. It takes a lot of skill to repackage the previous day's news from The Evening Standard. Sarcasm aside, I am a huge fan. You play a key role in raising the literacy level, so 'much props'.

Inveigle!

Ah, I hear you say, now this dastardly diary is about to get juicy – all diaries revolve around one theme and launches straight into it but oh nooo not this one. Oh well, what, do you expect from something titled 'Train Diaries'. I can't believe I've read this far and it's only about to take this direction. Come on, get on with it Ellis, you train spotter you!

Yes, the incessant flirting on the platform and trains might be the juicy bit for some and the females more than the males are the worst culprits. The females have it down to a fine art and can only be detected by a keen observant eye. You might have guessed it I take a keen but healthy interest in people and society.

Okay, back to these animalistic moves. Once they spot a guy with the features of a fairytale looking prince with a Roger Ramjet style jaw and the shoulders of that Greek mythological character Atlas, you know something is about to go down.

For all you industry types that can't define good manly features. A strong jaw and broad shoulder is the pre-requisite and features that scream hunk. Not eyes, not bottoms but a strong jaw and broad shoulders. Speak to the army they'll tell you it's the feature that defines and distinguishes the men from the boys. Not these present day offerings from supposed thespian hunks such as Hugh Grant and Jude Law. I mean, where, are the Errol Flynn's, Jim Brown and Denzel looking cats. Guys whose mere presence make ordinary blokes like us shudder and wish we could exchange our genetic make up for theirs. Leaving you wondering why your parents weren't specific with the Most High God on your physical attributes.

Oh yeah, Captain Flint of the Parachute regiment, my apologies. I wasn't injured when I pulled out of the 5 miles log race. I just couldn't go through with it. I kept seeing my mother's tearful face and hearing her voice as she pleaded with me not to join the army. Ah, those days when I harboured dreams of following my dad into the military..........

I digress. Now back to these flirting fillies in Ra-Ra skirts and Miu Miu peep-toes. Once they've spotted the objects of their fancy, they change the position they've hugged on the platform all week.

Gingerly but slowly they pace back and forth, all for that extra wiggle, desperately trying to gain attention. The movement is all but restricted to about four to five paces. This allows for a re-adjustment in stance when they‘ve stopped swooning around. The whole movement is like listening to the sounds of a military brass band. A huge thump from the Gretsch Snare and blare from the Brass Bugle ushers in the next move. With a slight tilt to the left or right to expose those child bearing hips. Cleavage heaved slightly forward to give it more thrust. Also while striking this pose; the mouth is slightly parted to accentuate the facial features.

Total movie magic, to quote my younger brother!

Every woman can now do the movie star pout but girls it is downright ridiculous, stuttering to expose the desired effect of any sort of allure. It just lacks the same appeal and panache as one pumped silly with collagen. Besides, those so called stars although they look just as silly, have practised their pouts in front of a mirror for countless hours, to get the distance between both lips just right. Every day girls just open their mouths and end up distorting their facial features and looking disfigured.

Don’t copy everything you see on screen.

If these subtle but aggressive changes don’t get his attention, she instantly develops a severe case of uncontrolled fidgeting. A full rummage through her bag, and frankly if you’ve ever peered into a woman’s hand bag, you’ll know that only a good rummage will do the trick when she is looking for an item. (In one instance, I’ve noticed a woman empty the contents of her hand bag on the train and once the guy noticed, she gave him a smile that said; dainty damsel in distress. The more aggressive ones just hands the guy a couple of items to hold – thus striking a conversation and bingo – he is in).

The fidgeting extends to her mobile phone, rapid texting and a telephone call here and there. The telephone call is always bound to get attention, whether it is received or she did the dialling. She'd make her voice sound sultry and interesting while letting the air carry the information she wants you to hear. For instance; 'I am having a quiet evening on my own'.

Although chatting on the phone is a potent weapon in her arsenal, since it gives you clues as to what sort of life she leads, it can't be compared with when she decides to unleash the piers de resistance. When she starts applying her rouge gently on her cheeks, or re-applying her lip stick, running her fingers through her hair with her eyes giving you that slight glint of affirmation that it's all done for you. Even a bona fide eunuch would feel more than a mental urge and crumble under such display of feminine seduction. The advice from the Most High stresses that, this is not an attack any man can withstand; hence He says 'flee'. Nope, a simple retreat won't do either, change carriages. If it is a 'strange woman', pull the chain and jump off the train it is certainly an emergency.

But guys, we just stay there, receive the smiles, let it boost our fragile egos and then act upon it. Next thing you know the visuals of her form are kicking-in and anything you can visualise you'll more often than not act on.

Hang on guys – stay with me – maybe the next direction will calm things down. This is not that type of diary men – word up! This is for education and liberation of the soul.

The women without tact, guile or panache will just smile. A very big broad smile with all the frontals showing – hmmm charming –yellow coloured gnashers – I think not! Guys that are not big on signals prefer it this way. Also they represent a sort of honest non-dangerous flirting. And more often than not, she would rather get to know you and only after you have been to the bar mitzvahs, christenings and had dinner with her Nan will you get to know if she slobs loud when playing tonsil tennis. This is why guys avoid these big smiles, run Forest, run; visions of a wedding dress just burst on my side, run she's really interested in you.

They all have an agenda but this particular one, wants to make sure you fit into her preconceived notion of what her man should be like. She has 20 copies of the step by step guide of how to trap a man and turn him into a lap dog.

Then there are some that get the wrong message from the suit and laptop bag. They don't know that the only image portrayed by a suit and laptop bag is only supposed to smoothen and enhance the passage to the boudoir not endless dates of 'meet the parents'.

No but in all seriousness, some of the ones that want endless dates of 'meet the parents' represent a constantly fading specimen of women with self worth that value the art of romance and courtship.

The same flirting process is employed when on the train. The movement is obviously restricted to constant swivels on the seat. It also allows for the Sharon Stone impression of crossing and uncrossing her legs. The applying and re-applying of her rouge and lipstick is always a stickler for me. The slow methodical application and the damn right suggestive double clenching of the lips to spread the lip-stick evenly, certainly enchants most men.

(But before I move on; a quick word to those women that put on their full make-up on the train, pack it in! I don't care how pressed you are for time. The train is not an extension of your dressing table or bathroom; so do it at home! The applying and re-applying of a few items on an already made-up face can be condoned but doing it from scratch is selfish and grates the skin of other commuters. In some cases the face ends up looking worse off than before they started the process of making it up. Trust me, I've noticed the disgust of other commuters and I urge you to wake up earlier so you could do it at home).

Alright that's sorted and hopefully they'll heed the advice!

The chattering on the phone while she sizes you up with a look that lingers positively making sure the message is conveyed can be quite unnerving for the guy caught in such a firing line. It is even worse if he is sitting directly opposite this vixen because she'll reel out the missiles one after the other until she is convinced that you think she is hot and your desires are on your sleeves.

The skilled and experienced ones make sure you are left a quivering wreck before they get off the train. I mean they unleash combos such as pouting, while stroking their hair. Eyes bent slightly downwards but systematically raised, so you get a full view of her layered eye lashes. Oh, and the smile is not far behind either – talk about sultry. With occurrences like this you might be forgiven for thinking that South West trains from Mitcham Junction to Syon lane via Clapham Junction is the Orient Express.

This sort of behaviour by women is not frowned upon by men, especially if they are the intended target. It is only when you are not, that it becomes totally and utterly distasteful. Frankly, downright inconsiderate, especially those that strike up conversations and start giggling, cooing and oooing – leave it out – we are trying to get to work.

The men do have some tact when it comes to the flirting game but with limited arsenal it's pathetic to watch. Only a handful pull it off, but those that are wet behind the ears, it's like watching a dog with his ears flapped down, tongue hanging out and drooling while the eyes just stare sadly. With 'if only' splashed all across his face. You haven't got a chance in hell, you're meant to exude the biggest aphrodisiac to women on planet earth – confidence. Or rather the appearance of confidence, as everything in this present day and age is a cheap imitation of the authentic article.

Counterfeits everywhere you look, from fake lives to fake body parts. Reality is now so warped that what is bad is good and what is good is bad. I mean even the English word bad when used colloquially means good – go figure!

Okay back to guys and their effort at flirting – it's only right I expand a bit on the chappies.

Basically, these guys just smile/blush straight in her direction, then read their paper and smile/blush some more. Ignoring the option of either 50/50 or asking the audience, they head straight for, phone a friend. "Hello mate, I am running late, about the meeting yesterday, I have revised some of my ideas and feel we should be decisive and implement them. The server can streamline all the information into one data source. I'll talk to Malcolm about connecting the Wis z Wig and short circuiting the portal. Okay mate, I am just a couple of minutes away, see you soon." This pointless conversation with probably a mystery person is done with a loud management style voice. She needs to know that I make decisions that can alter people's internet connection and crash their email servers.

If the guy has had one of those David Beckham style elocution lessons either professionally or by association, then he'd have mastered how to feed the right amount of bass into his voice. I mean if Barry White could become a sex symbol on the strength of his voice and a big band with trumpets blaring 'Tan da da tan da tan ooooh well, my everything, you're the first you're the last, my everything'. Then anyone can imitate the love maestro.

The ones with brass balls (hormones not under control and need deliverance) just approach the lady and strike up a conversation. Believe me, there is nothing more shameful than a guy trying to chat up a woman at 7.50 in the morning – atrocious behaviour. It's even worse when she buys it and starts smiling.

A quick example!

I was at Clapham Junction one fine summer day waiting for the 8.20 to Hounslow. I must admit I wasn't surprised.

During the summer months, testosterones and estrogens are visible on the skin of commuters. It just seeps out through their pores. This ratley (a street term for women used between, 1995-2000 only a few from that era still use it. Ladies, it's not derogatory at all. It just bamboozled girlfriends and others when it was used).

Now this ratley sashayed along the platform and took up her position like everyone else to wait for the train. That description doesn't help convey her appearance. She wasn't gorgeous but the ensemble was deceptive and projected a false image of beauty. Something ladies are good at. Well, they say 'Beauty is in the eyes of the beholder' and the men on the platform where doing just that, beholding her beauty, sorry, exposed flesh.

But to help your imagination along the way (now don't stray too far). Firstly, picture J-Lo's body with slightly less derriere. This girl was around 5ft 7 and wore a long white flowing skirt, that sat just below the waist line (stay with me guys). A white crop top that exposed her flat sun kissed tum and thin black chain that went around it. Around her long neck she had black beads and it complimented her black shoulder length hair. On her feet she wore black flip flops. Okay, now picture Trisha Goddard's face, because it will spare me the detail of trying to describe her facial features and lines. Although in comparison, Trisha is much better looking. Also the thick glasses she had on didn't do her any favours. Nevertheless, at 7.55 in the morning, a girl revealing some flesh and sashaying slowly on the platform is a fine sight. Also the white garment she had on, had you wishing it was the white sandy beaches of Miami at 5am in the morning with the ocean just shimming off! Ah the mind wanders, but I think practically all the guys gave her a resounding yes and thank you.

Now there are various types of guys, those that don't care and won't look and even if they do, are totally appalled at such display and exposure of flesh (Married for too long – although these guys become circus animals when apart from their other half or in their closest). Guys that look and just appreciate (happy relationship). Guys that look, appreciate and want to make contact but can't. (Loving partner but roving eye with an ethos of what ever happens on tour stays on tour) Guys that stare and contemplate. These fall into the category of rational thinkers. Thoughts such as, wrong time, wrong place, but my guess is, its just cold feet. And finally guys that, look and think it's done to impress them and make contact. (Every girl is mine) Oh and they succeed – punks.

The guy that approached her is obviously from the last category. He was dressed in blue jeans, slightly sagging at the waist, white T-shirt and black Nike trainers. (Guys I'll spare you the detail – ladies you're not missing anything). His looks had 'ordinary' written all over it and it's said with no pang of jealousy on my part – no broad shoulder or Roger Ramjet jaw.

This Pepe La Pue of the train station just strolled up to her and started chatting to her. No, he didn't know her from Adam. The frequent giggling and smiles gave the whole thing away and when they exchanged telephone numbers it confirmed everyone's fears.

It was one of those situations, where other bands of females vent their disgust at the recipient of all the attention. They show their displeasure with sighs, eyes rolling and sometimes kissing of the teeth.

Teeth Kissing!

If you don't know what kissing of the teeth is about or what it sounds like, ask a black woman to give you a free demonstration. The same goes for the black folks of Mayfair, Kensington and Surrey. I know that in your quest to climb the social ladder you've had to dispense of some cultural quirks and attitudes. I am also sure that you've stopped using chewing stick! So I suggest for an authentic teeth kissing session, you head to either Peckham, Brixton or anywhere they sell pounded yam, jerk chicken and temporozone in abundance.

Other cultures can learn this phenomenal sound but I think it's something to do with the arrangement of the dentition and the natural thickness of the lips. The artistry involved and the sound it makes conveys the full disgust of the person toward a particular act and it's dictated by the level of sound and the length of the teeth kissing. I implore you find a black person to give you a demonstration.

Actually, I'll set up a school and charge people to learn this teeth kissing, I'm sure it will catch on like whirl wind and set a new trend in London.

I can imagine it now, an interview with Ronke Phillips, although she'll be perplexed about this, why would her bosses have her interviewing someone about something her whole tribe has been doing for centuries.

The interview would run something like this:

Ronke: "So Ellis how did you come up with this new and exciting phenomenal sound to express disgust and frankly register a new speech pattern into the English language?"

Ellis: "Well Ronke, I was standing on the train platform when this plebeian decided to chat-up this girl at 7.55 in the morning. To register my disgust and disapproval in a coded way that won't get me the beat down, I incanted the forgotten African sound of clenching the teeth and letting a hiss escape the dentition to show and express my disapproval. (Then I'll go into some long speech of its mysticism and my ingenuity to translate it into every day speak. If female knitting clubs can be the new social fad –this certainly will).

You see Ronke, the polemics of this sound was first used by the African hunter to scare and deter others from his killing field. Back in those days, the sound not only warned them of your displeasure but if it's not heeded a sudden attack of what is known as the 'egelege' (or jack am knack for ground) will follow. Now the 'egelege' if carried out properly can shatter the backbone of another human being. Basically the sound of teeth kissing lets others know that you're displeased without the need for further conflict or violence."

I'll stop here, as my head is now filled with David Attenborough's unique but hauntingly nightmarish voice about African wildlife.

Back to the Platform!

The stares of disgust this girl received, implied that her morals where being questioned. If they could I am sure they would have grabbed the station masters whistle and blown offside; quick ten yards apart. Or grabbed the microphone and bellowed through the tannoy "cheap and easy" and the guy would 'get words' also 'what a dog'.

As for the guys, the shock that Pepe La Pue scored was just too much to swallow. If only we could ask him what he said – then we could use those lines. No it wasn't the lines, it was the way he wore his jeans. No no no, it was his stance. With the mind doing these summersaults, the arrival of the train was a pleasant relief.

The environment means that at any time of the day such behaviour must be frowned upon but in the morning, in the morning! Son you need to be sectioned off. At that time of the morning only the look and appreciate system must be used. Speed dating on the platform, what next platform txt flirting, platform ball dancing - come on!!!!

As I was saying, these people that I encounter on my journey. These ones that just about constitute the last fragments of community in a big city. These people that let you into their lives and homes with their loud conversations on their phone.

Technology must be given a positive mention here for its help in maintaining family and community life and gives us 'commuters' access into the lives of others. They mention names of friends, family members and disclose events in their lives – great entertainment.

Refreshing, hmmm but only sometimes!

Those that think they have to talk with such a loud voice – my gosh! I don't know about others but hold it down. Phone conversations can be done without the whole carriage having to hear you. 'Eh, Cherie, Raymond is going into the hospital to have that growth on his bottom removed. Yes, I know it's going to be painful, apparently he won't be able to sit down for months – poor sod'. A bit of consideration and decorum please. Also if you have to shout, please stick to only pleasant conversations that would appease and stimulate the imagination.

Now, there are those that refuse and won't relate or get involved with other commuters. Its head down, eyes buried deep within the lines of their book or newspaper. I feel these guys deserve a mention in this diary. To be oblivious to your surrounding and other people stands as a warning to folks like me.

Note to myself:

Don't ever become so insular and isolated within and without that I miss the wonderment and beauty in other people – no matter how introverted a character I am. After all, to quote Emerson; 'the invariable mark of wisdom is to see the miraculous in the common'. The common folks are all splendid treasures and it was on one of these, such journeys that I encountered a high school acquaintance that would take a common folk like me on a journey into realms I have experienced a bit of and want to experience more of. And how our lives are linked inextricably – yes that unseen director altered the script.

The Script!

Before I go any further I want to talk about this script business. I've already established that I subscribe to Shakespeare's observation of 'the world being a stage' but the question is whose script are you reading from?

Now there are various scripts out there, in fact thousands. The family, friends', cultural, societal, educational, historical, political, medical, financial, Biblical, religious, scientific, artistic, hallucinogenic, media and past experience script, to name but a few. God's script, fall into the category of Biblical but I'll buttress that by adding Holy Spirit led Biblical script; which is having knowledge of His word through His wisdom and applying it by understanding.

Which is the right script, I hear you ask and how do you know. After all, my script is dictated by past experiences, where I was born, my family background, social exclusion, religious oppression and incarceration, physical attributes or educational qualification. The list is endless but if you site one of these, you are still reading from the wrong script. Your life experiences and how it's been up till now should not dictate your present circumstance or predict your future. You need to change scripts.

The script lies in seeking God through Jesus Christ, the only mediator between God and man. Only then will you obtain the right script for your life. Basically your script has specific lines so you don't imitate anyone else but the Most High. Oh, and when you get it, remember to daily ask Him to help you master and act out His lines for your life.

Granted we are all born into depravity and inherit the customary pain and sorrow; some more than others, but in His infinite mercy and wisdom He set apart a particular day to show us His amazing love expressed through the cross of Calvary. Now at this point we can either receive the lines He has written for us, or ignore them and continue in what you think is the perfect script for your life.

You might say but everything in my life is going swimmingly, so why should I change scripts – the answer to that is simple; His script is the one. It is miles better than your present script and whatever script you bring Him, He'll improve it; with no auditions, criteria or qualification required.

I have heard that one of the worst things on earth is a person with a question mark over their head, basically not knowing who you are, your purpose in life or where you are going. (This has nothing to do with age, as there are pensioners with successful careers behind them that still don't know who they are, their purpose or where they are going). Only by looking at Jesus and taking His script will you discover and know who you really are. Until then you'll be spouting lines that are not yours and acting out scenes because of your circumstance and senses with performances that are laboured and heavy laden.

I mean some people take trips round the world to discover who they are (script) but come back none the wiser. All they discover is their ability to match Jimmy 'Five Bellies' when it comes to necking down hops, wheat and barley.

What I am saying is this: His script is the foundation and source and should motivate your every move.

Get hold of His script!

Nibble!

Okay that's the lightest starter you'll ever have. I am sure you're fuming and hungry to get straight into the main course. Tough, it is my diary and you just have to patiently let it unfold. It can't be rushed, just like whisky.

You sip it slowly and gently, if rushed, you end up with that awful whisky face and it takes a few minutes for your facial muscles to undo that horrible contortion.

This is the reason why some old men have those lines, they never learnt the art of savouring their whisky......... Also the surroundings for drinking whisky must be right.

Picture this:

A log cabin in the middle of a dense forest pervaded by a full orchestra played out by the sounds and singing of Owls and Nightingales bouncing off trees and absorbed by leaves, with forest floor Ant birds, Curassow and Sparrows buzzing their reply with compressed tones that resonate in the praise of the Almighty God, as it soars high into the air, delivering a glorious warbling tune that ascends vertically and then plummeting down horizontally to the approval and applause of every forest creature.

Inside the cabin, your velvet wearing frame is wedged in a solid oak dark brown rocking chair that's marooned in the middle, with a red and black luxurious blanket draped over your leg. To the right, is a fire place with fresh wood (chopped with your own axe) burning gently with a constant singe and spark to make your shadow glow and reflect all over the cabin. To the left, a Russian wick kerosene lamp, to give light to the wood carved chess board and its chunky pieces. In your hand a glass of single malt whisky swirling gently by the little arm movements that's controlled by the slight upward tilt of your head and grimace on your face from the after effects of each sip. Ah, opulence! Oh, let's not forget the lady sitting opposite you draped in soft light blue velour tracksuit with white trainers, a solid gold curb chain round her neck, gold teeth and huge afro puffs. Chin Chin – now that's debonair – ghetto fabulous!

Whisky companies you know you need to get me to endorse your product. I have just shamelessly plugged and made this drink cool – pay me! Oh and before you go over the top on whisky because of this trendy image, remember 'wine is a mocker, strong drink a brawler; and whoever is led astray by it is not wise'.

So you see, you have to travel with this diary and let every sinew of text, sentence and new turn unfold deep in your soul and spirit. This is the whole aim. To awaken, stimulate, intrigue, question and ignite your being............ Okay, since we understand each other, let's press on.

The Grind!

As I was saying, the constancy of commuting, voluntarily and involuntarily forces you to become attached to these people, the train, platform space, seat, window view and the signs littered around the various train stops.

The trip to work every morning and back is nothing but a big book of information that's streamlined into your system. For me, the source of news is not confined to just the pages of Metro. Every person or sign tells its own story.

Ring the alarm! Cliché alert!

Oh well, I had to drop some philosophy into trying to explain how this interest led me to the profound encounter with Idika.

I could jump straight into it and give you a blow by blow description of my encounter with God's son but I think more background info is needed.

My journey every morning starts at Mitcham Junction station.

Hang on!

My journey starts when I get out of my bed. I have got my routine down to a 'T' but I add variations to induce some much needed spice into my life. I am methodical but not obsessive and I like controlled chaos, especially when engineered by my own hands. Although this is never the case as the external assaults just constantly rage that I hardly have time to invent my own.

Oh, by the way, as you must have observed, which I doubt some of you did. This does not take the form of a conventional diary. We don't do dates and time but if you follow the story carefully, for instance the grammar, sentence structure and style, you'll uncover the not so cryptic chronological order it takes.

Most mornings, I wake up around 6am, aided obviously by my trusted alarm (mobile phone). Cold winter mornings are difficult to get out of bed – period! If only I could tow the line of those supermodels that don't get out of bed for less than ten grand, at least then winter months would be bearable. Ten grand to get up and wear clothes! Boy, I wouldn't even need an alarm! You can't believe how much I am forced to get out of bed for? I feel used and disgusted at the thought, if only I had their bone structure. Oh well that's that, but thank God I am still fearfully and wonderfully made and He has promised to review the amount I get out of bed for, so it's all good.

Once my mobile phone alarm goes off at 6am, the usual drill is to reset it for ten more minutes. You know that second deluded snooze is vital. The flesh, likes to think it's in control and thinks an extra ten minutes proves this fact. It is Mind over Matter (for those of you that read and question).But when you're living after the spirit, you don't fulfil the lust of the flesh. And laziness is a lust of the flesh. I allow the flesh these acceptable and harmless little treats and then subject it to a gruelling fifteen minutes work out of sit-ups and press-ups. Got to keep that six-pack in shape, this way I stave off any untimely attacks by the spread and its gang, adipose tissue.

All the hip folks, you know that all the rage is getting and keeping the D'angelo. What's the D'angelo? I hear you ask. Check the internet, ask a friend or look me up at the book signing or the various places my agent and publisher will have me plugging the Train Diaries.

I am not an exercise nut I just do the usual and eat like a pig. Blessed with high metabolism, you see. Now, let me see, I play football or used to (Can't find the time anymore – the stress of an executive role, I think not. Failed dream of playing professionally, no not that either, because I never tried, I just couldn't sacrifice my Sunday sleep anymore and my limbs have been battered enough by those lager louts that represent pub teams. Hang on, I did more of the kicking and fighting; fuelled by the on field temperament of Eric Cantona, the mercurial talent of Jay Jay Okocha and my desire to win every football game. But the main reason is that, I'll rather go to church and fellowship with The Lord Jesus and the saints). Use free weights once or twice a week for about ten minutes, then shadow box for another ten. Oh and if you include the ten minutes walk to and from the train station, that's about my exercise regime but it is constant. One word contains all the wisdom in this paragraph - go figure!

My Black Suit!

The morning exercise definitely wipes away any left over sleep, then a nice shower. From this point on everything is methodical, but I'll spare you the detail.

Basically I am always in a suit, my solitary black suit. Don't get me wrong I have two other suits. One beige and turquoise blue. I just don't think the attention they attract is worth the hassle and frankly my present status in the company does not befit the impression they ooze. The beige one was a graduation present from my mum, and it's a summer colour. The turquoise blue, I bought for my younger sister's wedding. I had to wear a classy and smooth suit to give her away. Something to make the bridesmaids and ratleys go ga ga.

Word of advice guys, a wedding ceremony is the most fertile ground to 'pull' – while this is not a diary of how to meet women, I thought I'd throw that in. I mean think about it! Every woman's reoccurring fantasy/dream is to get married and they call the shots, when it comes to how and where. Even the most hardened and militant lesbians can be pulled. But I am sure her wedding fantasy is so dormant that only a succession of visits to wedding ceremonies will arouse her feelings of getting married to a guy. The whole atmosphere is bound to stir up those suppressed feelings she had before her captivity and closest break out.

Alright, you might be pushing your luck with a lesbian, except you've got the proper anointing and stamina to cast out demons. At least you'll get to dance with her and hear her tell you how she doesn't hate men but just what they stand for. Then she'll give you a complete discourse of Shulamite Firestone's feminist doctrine and expose the stronghold that has her mind bound. (If only these present feminist, lesbians and women where as revolutionary as Shulamite's day, maybe they would have brought down the objectification of women in society, especially in the media.)

So my black suit is pretty much the workhorse. But to give it life and colour I compliment it with various nice designer shirts, sometimes open necked and sometimes with a tie. Now this complimenting issue would have been a chore if I had a navy blue, dark grey or brown suits. I mean who wants to be worrying about what tie and shirt compliments what. With a black suit, everything just blends. A nice dazzling white shirt and a red tie, oh la la! GQ all the way baby. Straight up mack daddy vibe right there, with the smooth fully drawn out.

Unlike ladies, we just don't have that much accessorising to do and thank God. It's hard enough choosing what tie goes with what shirt to worry about what colour of eye liner to use or what particular rouge will sit well with the foundation and highlight the lipstick. Not to talk of the constant re-applying at intervals allocated throughout the day. Never been one for women that go for those layers of make-up, but let me just say I understand.

Mishmash!

I have to pre-plan my combos' days ahead, it's important to co-ordinate but sometimes I wish I was like one of those guys that just get up in the morning and wear what ever they grab from the wardrobe. It can be mentally sapping to plan 'garms' and attires days ahead – blame the upbringing and this image driven generation. We have totally been emasculated! Instead of devoting our time to the advancement of developing countries and the enforcement of freedoms, we are busy pre planning what clothes to wear.

Even the baggy jeans, saggy pants and rugged set, although they'll vehemently deny any incline towards pre-planning of 'combos', they are fashion obsessed and routinely dress to match consciously. Since it is so ingrained, even the subconscious does as well. This is why sometimes you go through phases where you try to defy and break the mould that has taken shape by consciously trying not to co-ordinate and even that is an effort to co-ordinate – Aaah!

Or maybe its just vanity! That's it, pure vanity – after all the Preacher says; 'vanity upon vanity is vanity'. This blinged-out generation are only concerned with the outer appearance whilst the inside is at its perpetual state of decay and filth.

And this vanity alludes to the uselessness and emptiness of life which is not lived in fellowship with the Most High and in accordance with His divine will.

I am sure you're now used to these little bits of spurts of outburst. These diversions serve to expose a little bit of angst at society and its insistence on the outer man while the inner man perishes.

Foolishly and unbeknownst to these folks, if the inner man perishes, the outer man will also. The most crucial facet of your make-up as a human being languishes in its fallen state. And society constantly perpetuates and systematically thrives to erode any drive to rescue and improve the inner man. This subtle erosion by society is so rampant that all visible lines or demarcation of what is, good and bad, is somewhat lost in the bandwidths of summer. But before you cry desolation and total wasteland, help has been laid upon One in Zion. One so mighty that when you call upon Him, He is able to give you and bring that bling buried deep inside you. A bling that whichever way you turn the prism, it reflects, just says, flawless diamond.

On this particular morning, my pre-planned attire consisted of an immaculate white shirt, a red tie, my trusted black suit and one of those Ali Ba Ba shoes. You know the ones with the upturned front – diabolical design. I don't know what made me buy one as I always try to avoid trends. To crown it all, mine is slightly oversized so after a few street runs the front is turned up more than usual that even Ali Ba Ba himself will have a chuckle.

Before leaving the house I read and meditate on a portion of scripture and have some Quaker oats made with milk and eaten with marmalade. Essentially high slow release carbohydrate stuff for breakfast or else by 10am my stomach will be waging an all out war on the rest of my being, spoiling my whole equilibrium.

His Presence – my only desire!

The walk between my pad and the station is about 10 minutes and I walk very fast. I always opt to use the footpath along the park as opposed to walking smack dab by the cars and inhaling all that co2 emissions.

You're probably about to agree with me that going through the park will provide fresh air for my nostrils and lungs. Not quite. This park has a little river (River Wandle) that flows through it but I think it has off days. Some days the water stays stagnant, which allows bad odours to emanate from it. And the folks in this area feel it's a dumping ground for their beloved pooch. Picking up the droppings of their pets just hasn't caught on. I must say they lack the care and conservationist approach of the Wimbledon set. Maybe the introduction of a Starbucks will do the trick. After all it's a prerequisite and catalyst for urbanisation and civilisation. Who'd believe that coffee shops would play such an important role in society, amazing!

Now before you even entertain thoughts that my nose might be slightly upturned, I like Mitcham Junction and its flaws. Although I'd welcome changes to certain aspects, Sutton council administrators look me up. I have a few pointers but first I'd subject the councillors to the lyrics of Shania Twain 'you know a change will do you good', to help prepare them to receive and implement my ideas. I could mention them right now but that would rule out any effort on their part of contacting me and finding out what my proposals are.

My walk through the park is brisk and my being is engulfed in an appreciation of The Lord's awesomeness and love towards mankind. My conversations with the Most High, is that of gratitude and adoration. It's important to put things into perspective not just from a personal angle but also from everything that goes on in society.

In my teens, one of my friends died in his sleep. No he wasn't sick and the autopsy showed nothing was wrong with him. Africans are probably thinking death by 'remote control', they could be right but the point is he went to bed at night and never woke up. It is still very vivid in my mind, because when we turned up at his house that morning his mum said he was asleep and that we should come back at lunch time. Obviously, when he didn't wake up his parents banged on his door and had to break it down to gain access, only to find their 17 year old son dead on his bed.

The shock when we arrived at lunch time to find out that someone we had spent countless hours with and most importantly the previous 24hrs was dead, tore straight into the core of my soul and left an indelible mark, about the fickleness of life. The wails and screams that filled the street that day, was heart wrenching and traumatic. He only went to bed and never woke up.

On an even more personal note, His protection and mercy has saved me on numerous occasions, especially the most recent and horrific accident I had in December 2004. It is something that, when I explain to people they either marvel and thank God or shake their heads in disbelief. That day was one of those rare times when I decided to drive to work. That morning, I was held at the traffic lights on Lionel Road that leads onto the split between the A4 and M4 at the Chiswick end. Once the lights turned green I drove onto the A4 but my car spun round twice and careered off the road and hit a light pole from the side.

This is the disbelieving part for most people, no other car was involved nor was I driving fast because I had just come off the traffic lights. Also when my car had stopped spinning, I looked around and didn't notice any other car, person or traffic both on my side and the other side of the road. Bear in mind that, before my car started spinning other cars where present. I was totally amazed and shocked; it was only when I drove back onto the road that everything got back to normal. I went to work and told my colleagues but every one blamed the icy conditions but could not explain the solitude that occurred afterwards. I told my family that evening and they urged me to seek the Most High.

I was petrified to my bones, so I took a whole week off work to pray and read my Bible. (Funny enough earlier in the year, the Lord had asked me to do just that). You see, I always run to my Father whenever I have problems and stupidly go back to my old ways once He solves them. But not this time because up to this point, everything in my life was not lining up with the promises He made to me. Also everything I trusted and had faith in had caved in. During that week and the subsequent ones and up to this point, my Father gently explained, revealed and restored me to where He wants me to be: His presence. And in Him I have found everything I had been out searching for. Things such as; peace, love, joy, wisdom, character and success. Basically, I got handed back His script for me.

So during this time and with most times, I tell the Lord thank you for another day and ask for His help with my affairs. I have purposed in my heart to seek Him in all His effulgent glory. Not because of who I am but because of who He is, what He has done, continues to do and will do in my life.

So, it's all about reflecting His glory and letting His light in me shine through, so His love in me can touch others positively. Now, some days I'm so off the mark it's unbelievable but the cords of His grace gently nudges and pulls me lovingly back into His presence.

I have been in many places but none is as soothing, peaceful and loving as being held in the arms of The Lord. Then and only then is my entire being quietened – to just sit and gaze at His beauty and resplendent glory. Ah, a bliss that once found nothing else will do.

Lord I crave your presence continually. At night when I am sleep, you gently cradle and stroke my hair and in the morning your grace and mercy awakens my soul.

Maybe the words of this song will convey more explicitly where I've been and how He redeemed me:

I had wandered off to a barren land
Wasted all my wealth on the whims of man
Then your rod and staff drew me back again
Now my soul is satisfied

You have covered me with a royal robe
Spread a feast for me when you brought me home
Now I'm welcome here right before your throne
And my soul is satisfied

I was standing far off when you found me
I expected wrath but mercy flowed
This prodigal returned because you loved me first
Finding me, saving me

Now my only goal is to honour you
In the way I live, in the things I do
Let my life reflect all I've found in you
How my soul is satisfied

Let my life reflect all I've found in you
How my soul's at peace

And my heart is full of joy
Yes my soul is satisfied

Yep, I strayed but He found me and saved me.

Lord, but for your love and protection, they would have had me in derision.

Encounter!

Mitcham Junction train station is your 'straight-up' two platform train station. It provides a fast and frequent metro service into London and Sutton. Thames link services operate to Wimbledon and Luton. Also the Croydon tram link operates from outside the station, travelling either direction to Wimbledon and New Addington.

That last paragraph took more time than usual. There is no way you can jazz up a train station that is just bland. Believe me colourful words were used but how do you describe a place where the sky is constantly overcast, even in the summer. For all you smart Alecs, discount the people from this summation. The physicality of the station is what I'm talking about at the moment and it is flat. Even the words and characters of Reverend Audrey can't add colour to it.

By the way, the light poles on the platform have just been painted grey and light green, go figure!

I must say, most two platform station only have a ticket machine but this one is good in the sense that human interaction is involved when buying a ticket. It's serviced by a charming Sikh bloke called Harry with a distinctive Teddy Pendergrass (T.P). The discerning music fan knows all about this soul crooner. You young bucks either ask your elders or use a good internet search engine.

As I said earlier, I try to vary my standing position on the platform every morning and like clockwork, between 8am and the train's arrival at 8.05am, Idika just strolls along the platform to his standing spot.

He is always clean and immaculately dressed and has this look as if the whole world is on his shoulders. As he later explained in his dry and humorous way, he said: "someone needs to walk around with and portray the perception of having the weight of the world on his shoulders. It can't all be left to those incompetent law makers or the unjust. But what lies underneath is peace and tranquillity. The secret lies in looking longer, closer and deeper, then you'll perceive who's within."

For the sake of helping your imagination, Idika is built for speed. He is about 5ft 10inches with a defined but not so slender physique with everything in proportion. He has one of those manly broad shoulders. And from what I can recall during our time at South Thames College, although I knew him vaguely, the girls went ga ga about the boy and from all intents and purposes this is still the case.

I have noticed ladies on the platform and train give him those looks of; 'I'll do anything to make you mine'. Maybe the attraction is based on that serious look of his, because ladies love nothing better than a man in distress so they can turn on that maternal charm and nurse him to health. Before you girls concur read the previous lines to see that the look on this cat's face is not a cry for help but one of a contemplative man.

On closer inspection and true to his word of looking deeper, closer and longer. His soft brown eyes expose traces of distant but painful memories of spiritual and physical fights. His smile radiates love and reveals the face of one that has been taught and possesses the ability to be more than a conqueror.

Okay, so you've got a picture of my boy!

Before we got re-acquainted, I just wondered why this guy read so much and my first incline was to label him a book worm, but the dress sense just didn't fit the image of a scholarly fellow. I mean it wasn't brown corduroy slacks and tweed jumpers nor was his appearance dishevelled. Don't you just love stereotypes? Where would we be without them?

And it's not because we are now mates but he doesn't fit into my mini rant of 'these people'. He falls into the category of genteel commuters but like me has an acute sense of observation.

As I was saying, Idika strolled along the platform and stood at his usual spot in between what are usually the two front carriages of the train. He was wearing a navy blue double breasted jacket, black trouser and a white and blue striped shirt. His brown gloved hands held a small blue book that looked about 200 pages thick.

I must admit, I was eager to tell him we went to the same college and also I was curious to find out why this chap cut such a mysterious figure every morning. I mean, his level of concentration in his books made me want to know about a book that can rapture and demand that level of concentration. I read books but never with such intensity and concentration. Also my instincts convinced me that the look on his face and his entire demeanour portrayed someone whose life, has and must be just as interesting as the books he reads.

So, what's the deal?

The dialogue!

I shuffled close enough for him to hear me say; "How is it going?"

"Cool and you?" Idika replied and asked at the same time.

"Yeah, sound!" I replied ebulliently.

The seconds draw out in a long pause, luckily the announcer's voice came through the Tannoy with the security message of keeping hold of your belongings blah blah blah and that the 8.05 will be delayed by 5 minutes.

"Typical, when you desperately need to get in on time, they pull a stunt like this." Idika said.

"Yeah, a stunt indeed, well that's the trains for you." I said in my best critical tone.

"Nothing like clichés in the morning!" He said. I'm sure he was being humorous, as opposed to insulting.

"Yeah, they make the world go round. Not sure if you recognise me but I was at South Thames College at the same time as you." I was talking quickly to avoid any pause.

Allowing a little smile to spread over his face he said; "wow, I am normally very good with faces but hey that was years ago."

"Ten years to be exact, but I wasn't that popular and beside I disliked the environment at the time."

Idika replied; "shame, I thoroughly enjoyed my time there. Small world! So do you live around here?"

If he had stopped at 'I thoroughly enjoyed my time', I'd have labelled him smug but the fact that he kept talking defused any such thoughts so I answered, "yes, but for only about 5 months and you?"

"Oh about 4 years. Who do you remember from college and do you see any of them?" From his smile and questions, I think he was more relaxed now than when I said hello.

"No I can't remember names but I've bumped into a few here and there. Oh not sure if you remember, that very intelligent girl from Sudan, I've forgotten her name, but I ran into her in London."

"Yeah, I know who you're talking about but I can't remember her name either. She was beautiful and intelligent. I think every guy wanted to date her." Idika's smile broadened.

Smiling also I said, "I think most guys wanted to date her but were probably intimidated by her intelligence."

"No, I don't think that was the reason and if it was how childish. Except this was your reason?" He sniggered.

"Yeah, very funny and no not at all!" As opposed to being embarrassed, I found his brash but direct approach to be both sincere and without malice. But I had to change the direction of the conversation. College days where certainly behind me and I had no intention of reliving any of those moments this morning. I just never enjoyed my time there, despite getting on well with most people.

Before I could speak Idika said; “oh I did bump into that guy that played football for the college, not sure if you knew of him but everyone talked about his skills and how he’d go on to play pro.”

“Oh you mean Marcus yep the boy had skills and lightening pace but couldn’t finish to save his life. I saw him recently in Wimbledon, pushing a ‘Bimmer M3’”. Why I mentioned his car I just don’t know. I suppose that was what stood out when I saw him, awesome car though and as if Idika could read my mind. He said; “M3, nice! Masses of street ‘cred’ and presence – very nice!”

I am sure if the car was there he’d have been drooling.

“Great performance but I prefer the Alpina B3”, I was picturing those fat bumpers and grilles and if it was there I’d be drooling also.

“They are quite similar but the M3 edges it for performance and looks.” Idika said

There and then I knew this argument might go on forever, so I said “they were sort of born in the same hospital but of different dads.”

“Yes but the M3 is built for maximum attention, with more aggressive and bullish looks. Awesome machine!” I think from his answer he wanted me to agree with him as opposed to saying they’re both great cars.

Idika continued; “put both of them side by side and you’ll see that the M3’s stance and growl exposes its true character, compared to its more mundane sibling. It ripples like Arnie in a dinner jacket giving a speech – ‘I’ll be back’!”

He started laughing at his joke.

I was about to take it up a level by comparing its aggressive looks to a Porsche 911 GT3 or an Aston Martin Vanquish but decided to seize the opportunity to change the subject. Funny how we forgot about the college 'baller'! Ah, the Playstation generation, it's all about cars, gadgets and toys.

Then I asked, "How long have you worked for that juggernaut of a media company?"

"Couple of years", Idika said. But his eyes rebuked my inquisitiveness then he said; "what a small world. We went to the same college, live in the same area and work in the same company. Very uncanny don't you think?"

I nodded then added "hmmm" for good measure.

Another pause, then he said "and you?"

Holding his gaze, I said "about 8 Months" – my thoughts doing summersaults over his quick summation of the coincidence!

"The man doesn't use everyday words, juggernaut, that's a description that's straight out of the sea." Idika said smiling.

Laughing I said, "Well there's nothing wrong with being descriptive and verbose at times, besides juggernaut is apt for it."

"So what do you do for the juggernaut?" He asked.

"Oh, I handle the sales and marketing for various clients on one of our platforms, as well as working as a freelance journalist."

"Wow, versatile, what sort of journalism?" Idika asked.

"At the moment wrestling and a couple of other freelance writing." I replied.

"Interviewed anyone famous?" He asked.

Just then the train arrived.

Spot the Tash!

Some days you get those awful journeys where you are packed in the trains like sardines.

First off, just to get in, we had to go for a good old rugby shove. This is vital since you get people that are too scared to move in and stand in the aisle between the seats. So they hug the door area making it difficult for people with crucial 9.30 meetings to get on. I don't care what's behind their reason, of not wanting to get sucked in too far, whereby when it's time to exit they have to scream, push and cajole people to make way. Why, because people that are on just simply refuse to get off the train and make way for you to get off. They're also worried that they might not get back on.

Okay, I have successfully made an argument for and against. The only conclusion I can draw from this is hmmm – more trains – or just a good old rugby shove. The latter!

I had to stand so close to Idika and other passengers that it exposed flaws in Blair and Bush's shoulder to shoulder rhetoric. We are talking cheek to cheek. So close that I could see the pores and breaks in their skin types and pick out those men that use facial scrub.

But what I enjoy most is to play spot the lady with a tash. Great game, try it when next you're shoulder to shoulder.

Fabulous phrase of immense marketing value – I must applaud your spin at this juncture. It conjures up images of valour and dignity amongst men – but I think it belongs to that bygone era of valiant men on horse back or the fantasy world of the three musketeers. It is misplaced in the 21st century as it is shrouded in lies and deceit.

Wow – words – potent stuff, I tell you!

Okay, spot the tash, great game! These women with dysfunctional masculine hormones trying to cover it with layers of foundation; 'peek a boo' I see you. And to think I have male friends with no facial hair – ladies you should be fuming – I would.

Note to myself, ask a doctor what causes this hair growth in women – what am I saying, I'll use the internet.

Didn't mean to leave you hanging, so back to these women with tash, some would give guys a run for there money when it comes to clean shaves. When the next evolutionary process comes round (as if Darwin's theory is anything more than that – a theory) they'll be using Gillette's Mach 3.

I admire those women that brave the criticism and cynical stares and just let it grow, especially when they have only one stray strand of hair. There is logic to that strand and why they let it grow. If left alone it will only grow into a curly wurly, worst case scenario that curly wurly will turn into a thick hedge but in a dignified way and could pass for a Cindy Crawford mole adding a stylish if not demure look to the features.

Ladies with a curly wurly – heed these words!

Once shaved, boy, the result is nothing short of a full sprout of tiny hairs all over. I know. I once had a few curly wurly on my back, the same species as a female's facial hair. I stupidly listened to a friend, who told me that the hair on my back was unattractive and since I was going to be shirtless on the beach, the ladies would run a mile; even if it's a couple of strands. So I shaved those rogue hairs, after all it's wise to eliminate any potential female repellents.

Shaving those lightly scattered strands of hair was a grave mistake and it now looks like a corn field. With every shave the re-growth time gets faster. I think they're now obsessed with breaking their own record. I am anticipating that I'll soon experience a full re-growth once I've finished shaving and even before I drop the clipper.

These mutant hairs just don't like being touched. I feel the stray strand is their emissary sent to test your resolve with a Clint Eastwood like expression of; go on punk - make my day, just shave me! Ladies be afraid or else your lives will revolve around old spice, razor blades, clippers and Immac.

Ooops, no I didn't – yes I did say Immac. It's not exclusive to women, guys use it too. Okay that's a general statement, I use Immac to shave. But only on my beard and there is a rational explanation.

I can't believe I am plugging all these products for these faceless companies!

As a youngster I shaved with a razor but would habitually cut myself. My mother and sisters in their caring way suggested I use one of their products. I mean, I rub it on, chill for 4-5 minutes, then rinse and hey presto all the hair just falls off. Leaving my skin soft and smooth, so that's what I did. I used and continue to use Immac. Although the worst part is dabbing the after shave into my skin, very painful, because it opens up the pores so that once after shave is applied it stings like mad, but it beats bleeding by sharp razor. You have to use after shave as it safe guards against germs and bumps. Oh and a little bit of moisturiser also, as it preserves the skins' youthfulness. This is standard information but very few men have access to it.

I am sure you've noticed those guys that walk around with two skin colours and patterns on their face – shame. The reason one side is darker than the other is caused by the constant strokes of the blade. That amount of friction produces a different and tougher layer of skin to withstand such punishment. Dumb – stop attacking yourself in that manner. The companies responsible for men's products should speak to women, I think when it comes to beauty products they know what is best for men. Oh and putting 'gates' in front of the blade is a good way to guard against this sort of disfigurement.

Funny, at University I was embarrassed when my house mates found out I use Immac. I swore them to secrecy but re-reading what I've just written, it doesn't sound so bad. And don't think you can now market this product to men without my consent. I think it falls under intellectual property, so look me up.

Dribbler!

Since everyone in the carriage was standing shoulder to shoulder, I couldn't answer Idika's question until we got off at Clapham Junction.

"Phew what a packed train!" I said.

"It's all part of the grind. So have you interviewed any famous wrestler?" He asked again.

"Yep, quite a few but I prefer reviewing the live shows."

"I've seen a few on TV. I bet the special effects must be awesome in real life?" Idika said with a wide eye.

"It's something alright." I answered.

I thought I was a brisk walker but Idika could move. Also I am sure he probably pretends the other commuters are obstacles to weave, duck and dodge without breaking stride. I know a few football shimmies and fades are needed to go through the Clapham Junction tunnel but the faints and shimmies he was doing will have Ryan Giggs and Cristiano Ronaldo purring with delight.

Not one to shirk a challenge, I matched his stride, dropped my shoulder a few times and almost did a 360 spin but it would have been a bit over the top.

The 8 minutes wait, on platform 5, allowed for some more conversation and I think my display in the tunnel won his admiration.

"So what book are you reading?" I asked.

Most people instantly spout out the tale and complexities of what they are reading but not Idika, he just handed the book over to me.

The title was 'Knowledge of The Holy' by A.W Tozer. So I turned over to read the summary since no explanation was forthcoming. 'What is the nature of God? How can we recapture a real sense of God's majesty and truly live in the Spirit'.

"Wow, it sounds fascinating" I said, trying to get him to explain and expound on it just a little bit.

"I'll lend it to you once I am finished." He said.

"Yeah sure that would be great." Cool we are going to be friends, I thought to myself.

"I must warn you that although this book teaches about the attributes and illuminates on the splendour of the El Elyon, you must be vested in the foundational text of God's word. His word is the only foundation and authority on His attributes." Idika stressed.

"I totally agree." Finally he is explaining a bit about the book. Also the way his face lit up, exposed his most passionate of subjects.

"Don't you just love the way Jesus reveals himself to people? I'd never put you down as a Bible basher," I joked.

"Yes it is totally amazing how He loves and saves people, especially a down and out like me. Bible bashing is not necessary, besides, a word is enough for the wise. I just try and let the light He has put in me shine, so people can see my good works and glorify and desire Him for themselves." He said.

"I hear that, and since He is no respecter of persons, who ever calls on Him gets saved – period." I concurred.

"Your Sunday school teacher must have done a number on you?" Idika said smiling.

"Nope, I was the Sunday school teacher. I got saved in my teens and despite the fact that I strayed, I am glad He did it again. Both times He snatched me from death and I give Him all the praise and glory."

"Like wise, Idika said. And it's all done for His name sake. We are His witness that He is God and that He continually saves in spite of our waywardness."

"He certainly is a good God and I know He'll never let me stray again because this time I am making sure I don't turn to the left or the right." I said before he finished his sentence. I must stop doing that.

Just then the train to Syon Lane pulled up. Luckily no pushing was necessary and we found good seats. In fact I sat down in exactly the same position as I have done for the past two weeks. Great stuff when that happens because the seats have conformed to the contours of your derriere.

Personal ?!

“So are you married, any kids?” I asked Idika.

“No not married but I have two kids and you?”

“Nice. Never been married and no kids”. I said it with an air of invincibility, since I’ve never been a ‘prisoner of war’ or caught ‘missing in action’. I think he must have sensed this because I also heard myself saying; “baffled, two kids, how old are they?”

Unruffled, He replied; “my boy is 4 and my girl is 8 months.”

“I hope you don’t mind me asking.” I said and should have slapped myself for saying that.

“Funny when people do that, you’ve already asked and suddenly you have a conscience? No I don’t mind at all. So ask away?” He said without any visible facial emotion.

Slightly embarrassed, I couldn’t bring myself to ask anymore questions. I could stir the conversation away from all things personal and talk about football, work and the weather but they hold no new source of information. Although less intrusive, it is more of a coward’s approach and beside something in my spirit wanted to know where he was coming from.

As if he could read my mind again, he said; “No I don’t live with the mothers but I have my kids over the weekend.”

“Bummer, two baby mothers, most guys can’t handle one and you have two?”

"Yes I know but I rely on His grace to get me through and it is more than sufficient. And He has given me strong shoulders." A broad smile spread all over Idika's face when he said those words.

"I have friends that can't cope and constantly complain about how the mothers are systematically, no I mean vindictively and foolishly trying to exclude them from any involvement with their kids. Nor can I begin to mention some of the vitriolic riposte they've received and you have two women to contend with?"

Laughing Idika said, "oh well, in some parts of the world it's considered a sign of wealth, how about you, how long ago where you in a relationship?"

"I got delivered out of those types of relationship a while now." Slightly fuming, that I'd have to open up.

"Delivered, sounds like you were held captive." Idika said.

"You can say that again. You know those women whose 'heart is a snare and hands a chain'. I was the perfect description of a fool. And a fool in my book is someone that disobeys God's instructions and that of their mother. I mean I was warned by everyone about almost all of them but was too blind and stupid to see. I finally learnt the painful lessons but have no regrets from any of those relationships. Instead I thank God for the power to break free." Wow, that was easy; I thought to myself, I could get used to this sharing business.

"Hmmm!" Idika grunted.

I continued. “The Lord broke me free from so much emotional pain and mental anguish it was incredible. You know, one of those suffocating relationships, where every other day there was something to contend with”? Idika nodded! And I continued, “He destroyed my circle of one bad relationship after another and erased my ever growing mental list and my quest to accomplish it. The minute He set me free, the joy and peace that flooded my life cannot be described. So I am ever grateful to The Lord for another display of His power on my behalf.”

“So He picked you out of the miry clay and set your feet on solid ground?” Idika asked.

“Yes he did.”

“Those mental lists are a plague.” Idika said.

“You can say that again. Those blank cheques you receive and handout just lodges itself in your memory bank.” I said.

With a stern face Idika said; “obviously just like me you cashed and paid out on those cheques?”

“I certainly did, but instead of peace and satisfaction, I got pain and trauma.” I said solemnly.

“Total lasciviousness, if you ask me!” Idika said

“Yep, He saved me from enemies, who where too strong for me. A total case of the hunter becoming the hunted! On hindsight, some of those blank cheques already had my name written on them before the actual scenario. Even the ones I handed out where not all instigated by me, although it felt as if I was the initiator at the time. They were properly choreographed and orchestrated schemes with so much subtlety that even the writers of TV soaps would be green with envy; especially the ones that plotted and operated under the guise of just being friends."

Idika smiled and said "you know that now that you're living for The Lord you'll get even more blank cheques with elaborate schemes thrown at you."

"You don't say! It is even worse now than before, but I thank Him because I am trying to walk circumspectly so I am not ruled by mine or their desires anymore."

Idika stared at me then he said; "I think we fail to realise that once we know The Lord, we have to walk in obedience to His word. That's the only place we'll find peace, protection and prosper in the things we do. And also overcome those bad habits. But my biggest joy is that despite my short-comings, He drew me back in by His grace and instructs me in the way to go. After everything I have done and been through I'll be very foolish to want to pull back from such an amazing love."

I told him that someone said to me that no one ever backslided that was a 'doer of the word and not just a hearer'. "I mean, the Lord desires an intimate relationship with us. My conclusion from that would be to read His word, do what it says, pray and meet up with like minded people that would encourage and challenge us."

Idika's face eased into a broad smile and he said; "you know the Lord said; 'the words I speak to you are spirit and life'. So if we take hold of His word it will change and redeem our situations. To compound the measure of His mercy, He redeems then gives us an abundant life so that our earthly sojourn will be fun. Unlike before, when I was rejecting it and running away from the love of God, I am embracing Him and screaming; more!!"

I nodded in agreement and said; "I've found that knowledge is always asserted but once wisdom shows up, revelations occur and everything becomes new. The beauty about it all is that when I look into my past and darkest hours, all I can see is His mercy draped over my sinful and sorrowful figure. Even then I noticed that, He held out His hands to me, beckoning me to come.

How stupid and diseased I was, I thought I had to rid myself of my bad habits and be clean before going to Him. So I stayed in that filth trying to break free from things I had no power to resist or get away from. In fact the more I tried to give them up the easier it became for me to indulge in them and I failed at every turn and the cords got tighter."

Idika nodded in agreement and said; "that's why He wants to give us 'a crown of beauty instead of ashes, the oil of gladness instead of mourning and a garment of praise instead of a spirit of despair', (New International Version). Men, all we have to do is: surrender and accept the purifying work of the cross. And because we exchange our nature for His, we're infused with His power to break free from those things that held us bound and that so easily beset us. So we will be called 'oaks of righteousness, a planting of the Lord for the display of His splendour', (NIV). If He didn't want to save mankind, He would never have turned up – but He did because He knows that we can't save ourselves."

"Yep!" I said. Quoting scriptures, definitely a Bible basher I thought to myself and then said; "I have realised that there's no point standing aloof, saying I'll call on the Lord when I have sorted out my problems and broken free from all my bad habits. He would rather I let Him sort out those problems, besides I can't sort them out. So I seek His face concerning all issues in my life. And Idika, trust me He knows how to solve problems."

Right of Entry!

I was so wrapped in my conversation with Idika that I was totally oblivious of my surrounding and for the first time since getting on the train, I glanced at those around me. The man and woman sitting next to us were staring as if to say it was wrong to talk about God in public. I am sure they had labelled us fanatics. Personally I feel this generation don't fully understand that Jesus Christ came to preach good tidings to the world, heal the broken hearted and set captives free. So if this is the only way they get to hear a message that has not just been titled 'the good news' for the mere sake of it. But there is no better news anyone will tell you in your life time and it is even much better when you receive and accept the saviour behind the good news.

I am sure Idika noticed them but he just kept on talking. He said; "your point is true. We are certainly a stiffed necked people that trust in their own strength but the funny thing is we don't have any. I keep Hebrews 4: 15-16 close to my heart. Jesus is our high priest and those verses say; 'we do not have a high priest who is unable to sympathise with our weaknesses, but we have one who has been tempted in every way, just as we are – yet was without sin. Let us then approach the throne of grace with confidence so that we may receive mercy and find grace to help us in our time of need'," (NIV).

"Wow that's cold" (for you folks that are not down with the reversed meanings of street lingo. Cold means very good, extraordinary or priceless). Knowing that we had an audience and whether they liked it or not, they were hearing the gospel because it is the power of God unto salvation.

I buttressed the scripture he just quoted by saying, "You are absolutely right, that verse 16 refers to everyone and not just a select few. Let me just break it down to expose how simplistic His message is." (I was doing this so the eaves droppers could hear and receive this truth and you, yes you reading the Train Diaries, it's also for you).

"Let us: relates to who can go before the Most High; everyone. It's inclusive of all, no one is exempted. No special qualification, creed, status, race or geographical location is necessary.

Approach the throne of grace: meaning where we go; we are asked to come before the throne of the Most High God. The creator of heaven and earth wants us to turn up, unlike the British Monarchy where you have to be of a certain class, included in the honours list or come second in a sporting event and even then you might not get an audience.

How: he wants us to come with confidence and this confidence is gained by accepting and believing the work Jesus Christ did on the cross.

So that we may receive what: mercy: That line states what we are to receive when we approach His throne. I know He is rich in mercy because of how His love just keeps on flowing to me.

And to find grace to help us in time of need: relates to why. We need help with everyday issues such as; our children, relationships, people, spiritual, financial, emotional, physical and mental wellbeing. The list is endless and He knows we need help hence why He stretches out His arm inviting us to come before Him to freely receive what we lack.

What do we lack, some might ask, everything that pertains to life!"

Idika said "I like how you broke that down.

The WHO: relating to everybody.
WHERE: his throne of grace.
HOW: with confidence.
To receive WHAT: mercy.
WHY: to find grace to help us in our time of need.

A lot of wisdom 'bruv', thank God."

"Yeah thank God." I replied with my spirit filled with joy that I was sharing His message with someone that was just as passionate as I am about Jesus and because people are hearing it. I remember once at work, one of the very few times when I felt at liberty to share, I told a colleague what I was going through and he said; 'I never thought you had problems of that size because I didn't see any cracks'. That day I was angry at myself because I failed to explain to him that Jesus was the reason behind my peace and ability to ride the waves of adversity.

With this in mind I continued; "It's astonishing that when you read the bible you find out that the Lord covered every aspect of life. He never held back! He spoke about everything and to every situation and once received, it is effective and relevant in time and place.

Take nature for instance. He garnished the heavens with shining worlds (stars, moon & galaxies) and beautified the earth with precious things; so that all that is grand and useful, awesome and lovely, is seen everywhere in profusion. But would not a world less glorious and enriched have sufficed for man? No, no no: he possesses a spiritual nature, and therefore his Lord has generously fashioned his earthly abode to minister to the keen perceptions and deep sympathies of this nobler part of his being. Hence the exclamation of the royal psalmist; 'O Lord how manifold are thy works! In wisdom hast thou made them all: the earth is full of thy riches!

I mean because He made man in His own image and endowed him with a mind to think and a soul to live forever; He placed in his hands a book that unlocks His person, which would satisfy the mind and save the soul. For this two fold purpose He filled its pages with olden histories, interesting biographies, national chronicles, fascinating stories, lyric poems, sage proverbs, golden prophecies, astonishing miracles, beautiful parables, holy evangels, noble precepts, loving epistles, sublime revelations and other matters of transcendent moment, constituting in a volume which stands absolutely alone in the world."

Idika looked stunned and nodded in agreement and said, "To think that I spent years not reading the Bible and when I did, I failed to apply its priceless wisdom, I foolishly ignored it."

His face conveyed the shock horror of what he just said. I like this guy, his sincerity is on his sleeve and only the work of the Holy Spirit is responsible for such openness.

He continued; "it is the most authentic book on the planet and we ignore it. Oh well you know what He says; 'My people perish for lack of knowledge'."

I added; "it is the only book that when we read it, the author is present and once we ask, He gives us understanding and autographs our hearts."

I continued and this was directed to my fellow commuters. "It doesn't just teach us how to love God, but how to treat our fellow human beings and our business lives. God delights in His children and wants to be involved in every aspect."

Just then, the train pulled up to Syon lane, my spirit was totally elated, what a morning, I would never have guessed that The Holy Spirit had such an encounter planned for me – wow!

"So where do you fellowship?" Idika asked.

"Kensington Temple," I replied.

"Yes that's right Colin Dye is the pastor."

"Yep and you?"

"Oh it's quite hard to do Sundays but I go to the Apostolic Church in Hackbridge when I can and attend the Tuesday bible study group. You should pop down if you can, since you live in the area." Idika said.

"What, the one just on the border between Hackbridge and Mitcham Junction?" I asked.

"Yes, it is on New Road. The class starts at 7pm to 8.30pm, it's quite a lively session and either pastors John Quacoo-pome or Jayraj Nathan chair the discussions. You should pop down one evening when you have time?"

"Yeah sure I will."

Once again, Idika clicked into turbo and zigzagged his way through the people that got off the train to get to the stairs and cross the road. I matched him stride for stride and since my office building is different from his, we parted ways just before the entrance to Homebase' car park. I went under the tunnel across the A4 while he went through the car park and crossed the A4.

Nostalgia!

As I said earlier, there is no chronological order to this diary.

From that day, most mornings we'd meet at the station and chat until we get to work. Other times my boy will just say good morning, ask how everything was then read his book. This was cool by me, except I had to wait until I got to Clapham Junction to pick up the Metro. You guessed it they don't stock the Metro at Mitcham Junction station.

The morning when we talked about relationships, baby mothers and families, it was bitterly cold. I had spent the whole night itching all over, because these winter months have not been good for my skin. Black skin (my black skin) has been so dried up by this winter that baby lotion has to be used at least twice a day. I was feeling particularly melancholic the evening before so I wrote a short poem and when I re-read what I had written in the morning I was overcome with nostalgia.

I have revelled in the mystic
And enchantment of Africa
A place where the skies are laced
With celestial and ancestral bodies
A continent where the history
Walks side by side with you

Africa! My land
Will I ever see you again?
I remember your sandy roads
Cloaked in misty desert air
Dry arid ground
Pressing underneath my feet.

I have walked the length and breath
Of your house
Soaked and absorbed, but for now
I have exchanged your pleasures
For snow flaked roads and a frozen home.

But I think this reminiscent feeling was brought on by my itching skin because I have not been to the mother land since I came to Britain. Mentally and physically I have acclimatised so I am surprised I am getting attacked now, but it has been very cold.

To blend with the sombre mood I was in, I wore my black suit, black shirt and a black Louis Feraud tie with red, yellow and white diamond shapes all over it. When I met Idika at the station, he was in a navy blue suit and a pin striped light blue shirt. Since the morning wasn't as cold as the previous night I could flaunt my 'dapper dan' look without complicating it with a big jacket.

Idika's first words were; "what's up with you?"

"Dry itchy skin – you know the deal." I replied without thought for what I had just said.

"You should use baby lotion." He said.

"Men! That's what I have been using – fuming, people will think I have a rash."

"Well you are scratching so it is like a rash." Idika said laughing.

"Nope, it's not a rash the winter just dried the skin out." I retorted

"Yeah yeah yeah, you've got skin rash, don't blame winter," He said still laughing.

"It's the weather!" I said with a smile.

"Check this out, once it gets to autumn start using baby oil, so that before it gets bitingly cold like this, your skin would have been saturated in so much oil that you'd go through the winter without any 'skin breaks'." Idika empathised, I think!

"You are probably right," I said.

"Imagine! People will look at you in your suit all 'dapper dan' and smooth but inside your skin is just flaked out and dry – 'hammer tan' in London! If you go back to Africa they'll say you never left the continent. Ooohh 'hammer tan'!" Idika laughed.

(By the way, 'Hammer tan' is Nigerian 'winter season' and it is very dry.)

"Yeah, take the piss, so why are you full of smiles?" I asked.

"God's goodness" Idika answered. "I am under stress about issues with my kids but I've prayed about it and I am seeing my solicitor later, but your 'hammer tan' skin just cheered me up, so thank God."

Child's Interest!

"So what's the deal, you never told me how you got yourself into this?"

"There's nothing to tell, Idika said. They know and I know but what matters, is my kids and my access to them. I mean, why some women try to stifle men from being involved in the lives of their kids boggles the mind. Especially when it's a dad that loves his kids and I am not just saying it, they know I love my kids.

The fact that I have to go through solicitors or the courts is not necessary if the child's interest is always at the centre of every issue. It is of great significance to every child to have a relationship with their father. I'll emphasise the 'child's interest' not what the mother thinks is the child's interest. A solution has to be centred and applied around the child's happiness and a relationship with a willing dad is central to this happiness".

Idika continued; "I didn't grow up with a dad, so I know what it is like not to have one, I'll never let my kids grow up without one – despite the situation I find myself in, I am working hard to make sure my kids don't miss out.

Their attitude, reflect how myopic their vision is. Not just that, it is blurred by the self erected prison cells of bitterness and wickedness. Spurned and inflicted by their selfish motives. The short-sightedness is so bad that they can't see the damage it causes and will cause the child. If only the so called 'child's interest' was not premeditated by selfishness, everyone, especially the child, could navigate this treacherous start in life much better.

The wickedness is such that they don't even allow themselves the pleasures of going through the joys of pregnancy or motherhood. All they do is plot how to use the children to inflict pain. But the stupidity of the whole issue is that what they are trying to inflict is like a boomerang and redounds to them adding to their existing pain. The most important aspect is the effect on the child.

Okay, let's say the mothers adopt this other not so selfish reason. How about allowing the child see the dad, this gives her time to read, enrol on a course, take up a hobby, make friends or just laze about pampering herself. I think you'll find that it would create a much healthier environment for the child because the respite will ease her stress level. But the chain of bitterness is so tight, that they can't even see the benefits it brings to them or their relationship with their own child."

And he continued; "it is bad enough with the situations the children find themselves in, but some choose to stick to their selfish reasons and deny their own children their privilege and right to a relationship with a willing father. Using a child as a pawn is pathetic and their families and friends refuse to point out their erroneous mistake. Shocking behaviour I tell you – shocking!"

"I hear what you are saying. I play chess, so I can relate. More often than not, the pawn is the piece that gets taken first." I said with my face expressing the pain.

"Of course it is but this involves precious little children." Idika replied.

As if to redeem my last words, I said passionately but truthfully; "I feel that every mother should endeavour, if the dad is good and caring, to make sure the children have a relationship with their father. Encourage it, instead of stifling it. I applaud the ones that are already doing it, because they understand it is all about the children."

Idika agreed and said; "the ones that encourage it understand what it means to have the child's interest at heart."

"Maybe it is because you are not part of the deal and they don't have your love, so they deprive their child of your love and the child's right to have and experience their father's love."

"Perhaps!" Idika said rather impatiently and continued, "But they know they never had it in the first place and an act of desperation and wickedness is not love. It certainly isn't how you gain love. You can't buy this thing or manipulate your way into it. It is a free choice and both parties need to be willing participants all the way. But people use circumstance to manoeuvre themselves into positions where they have to be chosen. Instead of letting the other person chose them at every level, so that they'll be willing to go through any circumstance they create. Even if they choose you after the circumstance, they'll be choosing the circumstance and not you thereby losing out on their original plan of wanting to be chosen; which means both people settle for less than what they deserve; love. Don't get me wrong if both are willing to make it work by His grace, then by all means do so. I know God is able to heal every hurt and pain if we'll only surrender everything to Him.

But look my advice to every woman is that when you're planning your fantasy; about being with a guy for the long term ask him if he is willing to be part of it. It will save all the hassle."

Ah! a pause – I thought he was about to go off on another tangent! So I said "your last statement must be based on the fact that women call the shots."

"Well they do but men have their own fantasy also. We fantasise about casual encounters but believe me, there is nothing casual about it, even when you think you're on the same page."

Nodding my head in agreement and smiling, I said; "many have fallen prey to the fantasy of casual encounters. Rulers and kingdoms have been crippled by this fantasy."

"Oh well, but despite this, when the guy steps up to the plate and accepts his responsibility to his child, it should be encouraged. Whatever happens, it is the guy that loses out the most. Do you know what it is like not to see your child everyday and when you do, you know you have to take them back? Bruv, trust me, it breaks my heart constantly and I've only survived by His grace."

"You probably want more detail about causation," Idika said, second-guessing my question. "But it doesn't matter once the baby is born. The fact that you don't see your child constantly is a pain you have to deal with, then to top it all you have to fight to see the child for a day or two.

It is sad that you have to battle to get involved in his or her life and this is practically about everything and it shouldn't be that way. For instance, you have to force the mother's hand by taking her to court just to arrange to take your child on holiday. Something that's of benefit to the child or when you buy stuff for the baby just because the mother doesn't like it, it causes palaver. All efforts and desires to be part of your child's development and even institutional education, is met with hostility and resentment. All because you are not with them and this is even more shocking when they know that you weren't in a serious relationship in the first place. They want control so they expect you to confer with them about what sort of clothes you buy for your own child, but it can't be so."

In between him catching his breath, I said; "that sort of control stems from low self esteem and fear."

"Of course it does, but they forget that you already miss out on all the little changes, mannerism, quirks and a whole lot more. Also the child misses out on all your mannerism and quirks as their father. Having your child for a day or two is not the same and can never be. And this day or two is always under threat because sometimes they refuse to make the child available to you."

Letting my face empathise with him, I said; "it is bad enough and difficult for happily married couples to bring up children let alone when yours did not take that route." His face looked stern but I don't think he was hurting by talking about it, but sad at the situation and I sensed he was about to launch into another tirade.

"Do you know the first question my solicitor said to me; 'Do you have the emotional stamina to go through the long process and that I might not get the desired result'?"

"Justice wears an eye patch alright." I said angrily.

Idika nodded his head in agreement and said. "The government should do more because the children are the ones that suffer the most. Every case should be looked at individually because they deal with most cases based on past precedence of society's perspective of the woman being abandoned by the man. Some courts even subscribe to the archaic view that men are unable to take care of their children. I am not even going to dignify this second point with an explanation, because we know that men have adapted and can take care of their children, especially if their heart beats for them.

The first societal concept has been adopted because they go by the notion that every woman in this type of scenario has been scorned. (The preceding argument only applies to grown women) A scorned woman in my book would be one were the man and the woman sat down and discussed having a baby then the guy runs away once she is pregnant or when the baby is born. Or they are in a situation were they have mutually established the route and progression of their relationship. Then the guy disappears just because she falls pregnant. Then that woman would have been scorned. Marriages are excluded from this argument. But where no prior discussion has taken place or the nature of the relationship falls into the casual category and the woman chooses to in the hope that because of the man's disposition or how she feels, he'll come round after the baby is born, that woman has not been scorned.

Where the woman has truly been scorned, then that man is a punk. She is better off without him and he didn't deserve her in the first place. (To all you run away fathers step up to your responsibility, your children need you and deserve your input. Stop being a punk and be a man!)

In both cases, if the man is willing and genuinely wants to be involved in his child's life and proves himself to be responsible and consistent then this should be encouraged and facilitated by the courts and most importantly the mother.

It takes two to make a baby, so it stands to reason, however simplistic this sounds, that both should be equally responsible for the child.

They should speed up the process it takes to bring matters of this nature before a judge, especially where the efforts of a mediator have been exhausted.

Look Ellis, you and I both come from single homes, so you know what it is like to have one parent, it is difficult. So I wouldn't wish that on anybody's child, especially mine.

My advice to guys in this situation is that they remember it is all about the child's happiness. Keep a clean heart towards the mother of your child and stay focused on your relationship, commitment and responsibility to your offspring whatever the obstacle. How they turn out in the future depends on what you put in.

In fact this is to all fathers, there is no legacy you will leave behind that is as precious as your relationship with your children. You can build business enterprises from here to Timbuktu, but if you are not raising your children with love and a foundation based on the word of God – trust me, when that wind that blows on the righteous and unrighteous alike comes only those on the Solid Rock that is Jesus will stand. It says train a child in the way he should go and when he is old he won't depart from it. The operative word is train, not control, so make sure you plant and water that incorruptible seed that is the Word of God, because whatever happens in their passage through life, the root will pull them back.

So communicate, listen, learn, teach, encourage, admonish, explain, explore and most importantly have fun with your child, even when you are fighting to be more involved.

But enough of this, all I can say is thank God and to quote psalm 119: 71; 'it is good for me that I have been afflicted; that I might learn thy statues'. So it is by His grace I face each day and He certainly lavishes it on me."

Now that's what you call unloading I thought and then said' "You are absolutely right Idika. I used to think that enlightenment was based on education and upbringing but enlightenment can only be received from the Word of God, for this is where it resides. God's word if adhered to and applied will bring enlightenment to every aspect of your life. Not only to help you deal with the predicament you got yourself into but to get you out and keep you moving in the right direction."

My mind quickly wondered to how he got himself into the situation twice but I dare not ask him and I am sure the Lord must have enlightened him, just as He has me on fleeing fornication. Besides it would be inconsiderate of me, my dad died when I was a kid so I know how it must hurt someone who didn't grow up with a dad to go through the circle again with his kids. I mean that whole exchange had wiped the smile off his face and those painful memories that lie deep inside his eyes were so visible I thought the man would start balling his eyes out. Thank God he didn't because I wasn't in the mood to start consoling a grown man on the platform this morning, what would the other passengers think?

When the train arrived, we got on but the silence just lingered on until we got to Clapham Junction. Sauntering in my sober suit I was recalling and focusing on a rant I wrote about the lack of commitment in relationships. I was hoping to have it published by the Guardian but no reply. I probably lack the style and eloquence of George Monbiot. Maybe I'd have been published if I'd sent it before it was transformed to the Berliner.

I felt I ought to share my piece with Idika as it might help him a bit since he has been scarred and his is even deeper than mine.

So I said; "we are just people walking around with scars don't you think?"

"Yes, but you know what they say about scars?" Idika asked.

"What?" I asked.

"If it's a scar that means you're healed and the scar just serves as a reminder so you don't end up in the same place. And in the words of Mantis, 'we do this thing day by day and whatever won't crush us will make us more lovely'."

"Wise words!" I concurred.

Another silence and he started reading his book, so I pondered how I could use all this information to re-write my piece.

"I'll email you this essay I wrote on lack of commitment." I said to him.

"Alright cool," he replied.

Email sent!

The Diatribe!

Lack of Commitment in Relationship:

The whole issue of commitment in relationship is almost impossible to effectively manifest itself and be sustained. People in general are finding it difficult to establish and maintain any form of intimate relationships. The blighted forms of relationships include spousal, parental, friendship, mentoring and all other forms of interpersonal involvement.

This is an important issue at this stage of civilisation and it requires a collective consciousness to tackle this problem. It is not necessarily indicative of intractable pathology on your part or that of your partner, it is a process that is affecting everybody and is pivotal that we re-educate ourselves in the act of love and commitment.

Families are failing in their task to nurture and foster human beings that are able to develop any kind of relationship with people. This behaviour is wide spread and can't be attributed to dysfunctional families alone. (Besides the greatest dysfunctional trait happens when one is not continually connected to Jesus).

Government and society in general have systematically eroded commitment and love between humans. The selfishness of Thatcherism shook its foundations and solidified the trend of I and me, me, me. An example is the breakdown of families, lack of community and neighbourliness. This failure to develop relationships is now so endemic that we are unable to forge meaningful relationships because our underlying motive and drive is borne out of selfish desires. John Major's government of the early 90s identified this problem but failed to tackle it with his rhetorical policy of 'Back to Basics'. And the present one has opted to side-step the strong issues such as father's rights in favour of small financial handouts.

The so called nuclear families as we've come to realise, is also a breeding ground for callous zealots with a propensity for verbal abuse and violence. Some of these nuclear families are superficial and only endeavour to maintain this façade, as opposed to healing their rift. For example, such as fathers that feel that, just because they bring home the bacon they have a right to unjustly lord it over everyone. They expect respect but exude none and rarely instil any in their children. They fail to communicate and effectively discipline their children; in so doing, shunning their most important role in society. Or mothers that are never around to speak and instruct their children. Even when they are; the friendship role is all they opt for as opposed to being a parent that imbibes, demonstrates, nurtures and demands good character. For instance they fail to teach their daughters how to show respect and demand respect by their actions. Instead they compete with and manipulate their children while projecting their insecurities on them.

These families are producing, people without self worth, low self esteem or communication skills. They are constantly in search of affirmation and quit at the slightest obstacle that confronts them.

Other types of families contribute to the lack of commitment in relationships. Single parent families are on the increase, with a recent survey revealing that one in five children come from single parent families. These new forms of families are obviously products and a testimony of the failure of the nuclear family.

These children are given the wrong start in life, especially in a single parent family, where the mother uses the children as weapons to punish the errant male. Or in some cases they actually carry out their frustration on the children, emotionally, mentally and physically. The fathers are not exempt from this, as their lack of interest and failure to behave responsibly by being actively involved in the lives of their children perpetuates the problem.

Although the stance by the various pressure groups that are involved in uniting fathers with their children proves that, there are fathers willing to participate in the lives of their children, society is still feigning deafness and turning a blind eye. The sudden splurge and aggressive tactics used by some of these groups and fathers proves that this problem is at the precipice of explosion.

The government and the law have failed these families, especially the children. In most cases they can't get a redress in court and when they do they can't be enforced.

There are so many reasons for this huge growth in single parent families. The most obvious is the lack of love and commitment. The quest for love in society has the same tendencies and correlation with the pursuit of wealth and success. People do whatever they can to get both but end up with nothing. Ladies get pregnant regardless of whether the guy loves them or not. Men and women fail to use contraception or define the parameters of the relationship. The latter is irrelevant as some women are aware of the parameters but assume a child will change everything. It certainly changes everything but never the desired outcome.

Not all single parent families are borne out of deception or the need to trap a partner. Some find themselves in this position due to the disappearance of an irresponsible and selfish partner, poverty, violence in the nuclear family or the death of a spouse. More often than not, the children grow up with the emotional pain passed onto them by either of their warring parents or a lack of love in the home. They develop phobias and grow up not having the emotional ability or the necessary social skills to engage in a loving relationship.

The daughters settle for any male that shows them affection, because they're unable to distinguish and identify genuine affection or character. The sons cannot express love to one woman, although with this age of heightened promiscuity both sexes depict and exhibit similar character traits of promiscuity.

For the male child it might be because, he has been the emotional pillar for his mother's failed relationship. He knows her pain is caused by men or the lack there of and it makes it impossible for him to sustain any long term bond with women. One aspect would be fear of getting too close to females so he doesn't hurt them. Another aspect would be having too many women in his life because he feels he is the only one that can really care for them since he is always loyal to his mother, the conflict is always too great and he sees no reason to have a committed relationship with any other woman. He is forever, needed by his mother.

All this might sound very Freudian, but people are growing up with in-built defence mechanism, that is opposed to commitment. For instance, majority of 21-35 year olds will rather co-habit than get married. Preferring to shun a God ordained institution, in favour of a flexible relationship. Basically, what this means is that they have a get out clause at the first sign of trouble. Although arguments can be put forward that marriages nowadays break up just as fast. But this is due to the motive by some of the couples involved and they lack the proper foundation or preparation for marriage.

In the early 90s I'd have argued that the arrangement of co-habitation favoured the men more than the women, but this is not the case. Both sexes are almost now on the same level playing field.

The men favour it because they have the security of a woman at home (sex on tap, emotional companion and a lady to look after them – if she has maternal tendencies) and the freedom to opt out. It is also financially viable. The women favour it because they can still hold on to their dream that one day he might propose and if he doesn't we already live together like a couple. A nice way to ease him into the habit and idea of being married, just the right amount of pressure will make him realise that it is not a bad option. They are willing to be patient and nudge him gently down the aisle. And it gives her the chance to see if he is the right one for the long haul. This aspect also gives them the freedom to opt out when it gets rough.

Although a start, co-habiting is not the answer to commitment and love. Half the time it is shrouded in deceit, peer pressure, infidelity, emotional insecurity, possessiveness, convenience and hidden agendas to drag someone down to the Alter. Nobody interacts or make their feelings known. They go with the flow and compromise to the point where they lose any sense of identity.

However co-habitation is packaged it is still a form of marriage (in society but biblically it is wrong) but without the tone of finality. The roles played by both male and female are similar and it is just as devastating when it breaks up, but it lacks dignity and honour. In a marriage at least both sets of parents have been given due acknowledgement that their daughter or son is loved enough for me to do the honourable thing. And most importantly you have both established that you love yourselves enough to want to be together, instead of hiding behind an imitation while professing undying love. Arguments of 'we don't have to prove our love to anyone', has no bearing and neither does a long 10 year engagement. You are already doing that by living together and settling for less than your original dreams. But like I said earlier, it is used to test the waters but with co-habitation it is as if you are getting them on the cheap.

In the majority of both kinds of this relationship the true foundation of love is not in place and expectations are not explicitly communicated or understood.

Never have there been so much focus on people and how they interact, as it is now. The multitudes of self-help books and the media's constant scrutiny of the lives and relationships of celebrities are also a catalyst for lack of love and commitment. We're intrigued by their lives to the point where it gives us pleasure, makes us jealous and acts as a yard stick for our relationships. More often than not people and the celebrities that are put on a pedestal and imitated don't have the spiritual vigour, tough mindedness, emotional stability or physical stamina to live up to these expectations.

Debased morality, dysfunctional family unit, so called celebrities, the media and long working hours are all part of the root cause of this decay and stagnation in relationships. Basic relationship with families and friends has been reduced to festive holidays, birthdays and the now defunct day for lovers: February 14th. I say defunct because Valentine's Day has evolved into a commercial farce with elaborate romantic schemes. More often than not it is done so people can brag about how loved they are, only to return to the quagmires of expressionless love. In fact very few know the story behind St Valentine's Day.

The last four decades and the attitudes of those before us are also to blame. The 60s crippled and reduced relationships to sporadic and scripted encounters. Basically if the feeling inside is not cosmic, a drug infused euphoria or does not pull at your heart strings like the electro cords of Jimi Hendrix' guitar, then it's not love.

The influence of the movie industry ensures that everyone aspires to have a relationship as romantic as 'Sleepless in Seattle' or 'When Harry Met Sally'. There is nothing wrong with desiring these utopian and sometimes imaginative love scenes, but the standards are too high. People don't have the time, capacity or aptitude to develop and sustain a romantic relationship of this magnitude. Even if it starts out beautifully, no one is prepared to stay and fight when things go wrong. The grip of selfishness in humanity is such that everything is now one strike and you're out.

Another obvious resistance to commitment is contraception. This is also a legacy of the sixties, hence the phrase "free love". They revelled in the freedom and to some extent the equality between sexes. I am not opposed to the positive aspects, such as prevention of sexually transmitted diseases, unwanted pregnancy and the liberation it gives women and men. It is the negative effects it's had on society and commitment that I am talking about. Basically promiscuity in both sexes is now at epic proportions. The publicity and acceptability of such behaviour has certainly incapacitated commitment. Instead what you have are variants and diluted versions of what commitment is.

The 70's, offered psychedelic behaviour and the complete breakdown of the family unit. Divorce rates increased and single parent families became the norm. Women around the world were heeding the revolutionary chants of feminism and taking action against unworthy, controlling and evil patriarchs. Obviously with each breakdown having its own distinct problem and out come.

The 80's left nothing to be desired. The music was decadent, loud and without harmony. The fashion a riotous combination of sheer bad taste and the governmental policies of the day were not in favour of families. The only altruistic event worth mentioning has to be Bob Geldoff's quest to feed the world through Live Aid!

The 90's had the entire world gripped in the hysteria of the world coming to an end. With references to Nostradamus and his vision, it fostered more greed and infused what started in the 80s. People did things without any sense of remorse and shunned commitment in favour of having numerous partners.

It also saw a huge advancement in technology, the internet and mobile phones being the most innovative. Although it has positive aspects, it has also played a part in stifling relationships. Their rapid growth and use have depersonalised relationships and commitment.

I am not the moral guardian of society or a saint just a product of my environment, but I am daring to be different. This lack of love and commitment is making people settle for less than they deserve. People put up with 'wife and husband beaters', serial womanisers, kings and queens of infidelity. And the answer to this is simple, people want to love and they want to be loved. Everybody is engulfed and obsessed with love, so they take whatever they find and are grateful, half the time this is unrequited love. For some when they find a good thing they are too blind to see it and take hold of it.

Pondering his response!

That day I was so busy and got called away so I didn't get a chance to go back to work. Oh well I'll see his views on it, tomorrow.

The next morning, I was so eager to find out his insights and suggestions that I sprinted through the park and 'bummer' he wasn't at the station. I am not one for suspense and the Lord is still teaching me patience in all aspects.

Phew! Two minutes later just as the train was pulling into the station, I saw Idika jugging gingerly.

"You're a lucky boy!" I said.

"Blessed of the Lord you mean," he said.

I smiled, "so what did you think of my essay?" Jumping straight in!

"I sent you an email yesterday, didn't you get it?" He answered and asked.

"No I was out of the office all day, so?" I asked impatiently.

"What? You know you can wait and find out when you get in, instead of behaving like a woman and bugging me this morning," Idika said with a smile.

"Come on, I am thinking of having it published. So let's hear it."

"Alright – chill! In my email I said, it was an interesting, bold and heartfelt essay. You might be touching on one of society's core problem."

I think he probably knew I wanted him to say more, so he said; "Yo men! It is a bit disjointed but very good; you've got skills!"

"Cheers, but I feel it needs to flow better and there is something lacking. I don't think I explicitly explained why relationships breakdown or the solution?"

Love!

"Well, since you asked, Idika said. The solution and answer to all man's problem reside in Jesus Christ. The creator is the only one that can fix His creation and He has given the sons of men the road map to solving every problem. The answers are in His word and in seeking Him.

God is a spirit, so it stands to reason that all our problems and answers are spiritual. Jesus said the words I speak are spirit and life. The solutions are in His word and if it is not your base or motivation, all you'll produce will be variants of His truth. And Ellis, variants lack substance and authenticity.

Take your subject matter for instance 'lack of love and commitment' the reason it is failing is because the enemy; Satan, is trying to distort and stifle God's original intention for His creation. He has been deceiving people for ages, lying to them that they can maintain a healthy relationship despite neglecting their relationship with The Most High.

The only commandment Jesus gave, I think it's found in Matthew 22: 37-40 'Love the Lord your God with all your heart and with all your soul and with all, your mind. This is the first and greatest commandment. And the second is like unto it: Love your neighbour as yourself'. We have to continually make sure our relationship with Him is growing in love and in doing so our relationship with those around us will flourish and this will lead to a better understanding and love for ourselves.

Selfishness is rife in all forms of relationships, including our relationship with The Lord. Self has to be dethroned and beheaded because it has since conspired with the devil to usurp God's throne in our hearts. We worship a god that we've reduced to fit into our schedules and passions. But the God of the universe does not conform to our reason or intellect. He is greater than the mind and must be worshipped in spirit and truth. And this is the kind of worship Jesus told the woman at the well that the Father wants. His word is spirit and truth and only by submitting to the Holy Spirit will we be taken into all truth. It is on His terms not ours and I'll stress it again Ellis His way is the best and perfect way."

"You are right, I said and added; the door to God is guarded by that proud spirit of self and reason and this has to be vanquished. All it takes is for us to confess our sins and daily submit in humility to the Most High who is of absolute necessity to everyone."

"Yeah I like that Ellis! God is absolute necessity for all. He said 'I am the way, the truth and the life' not I know the way, not I know the truth and certainly not some life. But a categorical 'I am the way', an uncompromising 'I am the truth' and a resounding and emphatic 'I am the life'. So how dare you try to have any of this without him?

You want love! It says God is love! The difference is people have love but God is love. Our love comes and goes depending on how we feel or how people treat us, while God's love stays the course. It is steadfast and eternal. I mean, we have scaled the heights of technology, climbed to the mountain peaks of academia and are forever pushing the boundaries of medical science but we can't live with each other or raise children that are capable of love – very sad!

To fully operate in love, and I am talking of His selfless love, we have to be continually linked to Him; the source of love."

To buttress the love he was talking about, Idika quoted first Corinthians 13 to further expound on its qualities, Idika said:

Love is patient
Love is kind
It does not envy
It does not boast
It is not proud
It is not rude
It is not self-seeking
It is not easily angered
It keeps no record of wrongs

Love does not delight in evil
But rejoices with truth
It always protects
Always trusts
Always hopes
Always perseveres
Love never fails.

And he continued. “Once you accept Jesus as your Lord and saviour, the Holy Spirit empowers you to love God and encourages you to channel and display this love you’ve found in Him to your neighbour, as well as teaching you to love yourself.

I use the word encourage because it’s our choice to love our neighbour as ourselves, but be warned that when you don’t, you harm, hinder and stifle your relationship with Him. And no person is worth that at all. He has forgiven me, so I forgive people that hurt me by His power.

Men! The peace and joy I’ve found in Him, is too priceless to throw away or lose even for one split second. Ellis, I know this, not by mental ascent but by His divine revelation. I urge you to constantly go beyond the threshold of mental ascent and continually ask Him for an encounter that will revolutionise your entire life and reveal His person.

Ellis, only His presence will do in my life and that’s all I seek. So I aggressively pursue and thrive to stay where He has put me. Only then will the qualities of love in Corinthians 13 be conceived, established, projected and exercised in my everyday life. I have to move with Him as He takes me through the process. Sometimes it is hard especially when people deliberately hurt me but I want to be close to Him, so I endure by submitting myself to His will and holding fast to His words in me.”

“I feel you, but we count it all joy”. I said and added. “Funny though the scripture you just quoted is read in most marriage ceremonies but nobody bothers to find out how to put it into practise. I suggest that at the rehearsals, they make the pending couple learn and understand what it means to love and to know about the author of love. We confess love everyday but flap at expressing it because the qualities and requirements of love are not known or understood.

Surely only Adam and Eve were privy to love at first sight. We on the other hand, have to learn about love and commitment and make use of its organs properly. The reason I am saying this, is that people feel that once they like the physical attributes of a person then it is love. Just sharing a glance, smile and then cooing at each other for two weeks is not love, but an attraction of the senses. There is nothing wrong with it but love is a symbiotic process that involves learning, exchanging, compromising, retuning and the merging of the body, soul and spirit."

"I like your description about it being a symbiosis because it is an interaction between two different organisms living in close physical association to the advantage of both." Idika added.

"Certainly, it is mutually profitable to both. That's why the Lord said humans, especially couples should submit themselves one to another; but we don't fully understand or operate in it. The feminist and career minded female thinks it's another avenue for the sceptre of male dominance to flex its muscles in their affairs. The chauvinist and traditional male think it gives them the right to control and lord it over the woman. And those folks in the middle think it calls for passivity and to some extent servitude in the relationship.

They are all off the mark! Submitting yourselves one to another is an empowerment to allow each person to be all they can potentially be in life and in that union. This will redound to His praise and glory."

"This process is made easier if His word is active in you." Idika said and added, "Let me just squash this argument once and for all before you continue with your point on love and commitment.

No human should dominate or control another. God made us for rulership but because it is a delegated power we have to be in tandem with His counsel. We have the ability to rule over everything in nature but never over another human being and if you are doing this you are in direct violation of a spiritual and natural law.

Manipulation and control is another example of human dysfunctionality. The folks that engage in this do so because of their shortcomings. They can't rule over their emotions, flesh or life in general and out of fear try to rule over others to establish this sense of rulership. They are aware of this quality within them but don't know how to activate it or exercise it. Ellis, fear schemes, intimidates and manipulates and is evident in all kinds of relationships. From the work place to the home, even the playground. In the work place bosses and colleagues are forever trying to use their position to rule others, especially the weaker ones. At home spouses use manipulation and intimidation. Parents try to control their children instead of training them in right and wrong and living exemplary lives. Some are too scared to honestly admonish for fear that their children might say they don't love them. The children in turn, use the same inherited fear and manipulation on their parents. In the playground friends do exactly the same as the work place. But love on the other hand, has no fear in it. Those that fear or are ruled by it have no love in them and are not made perfect in love. But if they let love move them, they'll see that they don't have to dominate or control anyone because love is very attractive and releases a fragrance that people naturally gravitate to."

"You are absolutely right. As I was saying; take the word commitment for instance, it means; "the act or process of entrusting or consigning for safe-keeping, or the state of being bound emotionally and intellectually to a course of action or to another person. And words such as promise, pledge, vow, assurance, loyalty, dedication, devotion, faithfulness, allegiance and staunchness are closely related to it and buttress its meaning. Once you get an understanding of these words, it will curb how you bandy the word commitment around and also it might help you re-evaluate your present relationship."

Exactly Idika said. "Some folks don't know that one of the offshoots of commitment and love is honour. They also say 'to honour' at weddings, but for most of them nothing in their relationship suggests that they give or receive honour. To love is to honour and it has implications which spell out that you have to go out of your way to find out and carefully prepare and do things that will elevate, remind and bring pleasure to the other person. It's like The Lord saying 'If you love me you'll keep my commandment'. Therefore we have to find out what He says and what pleases Him and obey Him, because obedience glorifies God.

Basically, to love and honour is to indulge in the meticulous search of everything the other person is and likes and this is a life time task that requires all the other facets such as patience, trust, hope and perseverance to be active."

“I hear you, but the reason why people are off the mark is because they fail to realise that love is indivisible from life. They don’t know Him neither research Him diligently. Therefore don’t know who they are and neither do they have the ability to see their partners for the person he or she truly is. Nobody takes time, just like you’ve said to meticulously seek God or the true character of their spouse.” I said.

“Ellis, it’s all down to our inherent selfish nature and we have to daily choose to live by His word. The complexities and depth of one’s partner should keep one inflamed with love and longing for the rest of one’s life. Especially if one knows and learns how to fan the flames of passion into the relationship. Make disclosure a priority and earnestly seek out their strengths and faults. And most importantly, individually and collectively chase after the Most High, because as you do, He’ll lead you to the true nature of yourself and your spouse. The end destination for a couple is oneness in spirit, soul and body just as we are destined for oneness with Him when we are re-born of His Spirit.” Idika said.

“What I am about to say is slightly trivial but you’ve just exposed the flaws of my past relationships. Some of them confessed undying love to the point of tears but didn’t even know my middle name. I mean no effort to find out about the person they say they love; more importantly for their own peace of mind, because claims and schemes were rife about wanting to spend the rest of their lives with me.”

“Sad but did you know theirs?” Idika asked.

“Yes I did but failed them at other aspects such as commitment, so touché. What I am saying is this; love in its entirety must be acted out. Saying it from dawn till dusk does not give it substance. Acting it out does and makes it more significant.

Okay take for instance those sadistic imbeciles that say they love someone but conduct their relationships based on that saying 'Treat them mean keep them keen'. These people are not in love and don't know love, because love has no guile or inferiority complex. It is pure and always wants the best for the one it is directed at. God's love is one hundred percent pure."

"Ellis, it's just like what you said. We don't fully understand even the dictionary meaning of commitment or love let alone that of The Most High. A love that is eternal in nature and active in time. We only concentrate and profess the aspect of love that satisfies our emotions and flesh. And refuse the other symmetrical facets such as devotion, respect, admiration and appreciation.

Due to our spiritual blindness and natural ignorance, we fret constantly about not being loved by either God or man; especially those in relationships. But God can't be blamed because His love has been revealed and our constant rejection of it produced and produces impatient, insecure, nervous and anxious people, whose daily lives are ruled by fear.

And we wonder why there is a lack of love in society. We need Him – He is love. He freely gave so that when received we would freely give. We can't earn or buy love, it is free and nothing outside of you should motivate love to flow. Just as nothing outside God motivates His love to flow, because we certainly don't deserve it. But it is God's nature and essence and when you live in His kingdom, love should and must become your essence and nature.

Check this out, in your spare time read 1 John Chapter 4, in fact read the whole of 1 John, it talks a lot about God's love and how we are to love each other."

As Idika spoke, I felt the presence of The Holy Spirit embrace me like a big blanket. My whole being was filled with goose bumps and I felt a unity in my being that words fail me to put into context. My eyes welled up with tears and my heart was lifted up in adoration of Jesus. My Lord how you love me and reveal yourself to me – you have placed your hand upon me, such knowledge is too wonderful and too lofty for me to attain. My God, you called a wretch like me into your presence. Lord, I'll have nothing if I lose your presence. Your hands have made me and fashioned me; give me understanding that I may know you better?

The words Paul wrote in Philippians 3.10 flooded my heart; 'My determined purpose is that I may know him, that I may progressively become more deeply and intimately acquainted with him; perceiving and recognising and understanding the wonders of his person more strongly and more clearly'. (Amplified Version)

When the train pulled up at Clapham Junction I was just about to bust into my stride but Idika stopped and said: "Wow, I don't know if you felt His presence but it was awesome?"

"Oh yes, I bless and praise His Holy name." I said.

Wisdom!

Then he said, "you know what you said the other day about enlightenment, you are absolutely right. It has nothing to do with education, upbringing or status but everything to do with the Word of God. The entrance of it gives light and understanding to the simple.

I have been in the buildings and even entered the crevices of worldly enlightenment. I have encountered and conversed with learned and scholarly fellows that hold court in the pantheons of academic achievement, corporate entities and watering holes (bars). Most of them, lack true enlightenment. They are puffed up because they have worldly knowledge. They fail to realise that knowledge without wisdom is deceitful and delusional. And as explicitly argued by Rod Parsley in his book, 'Silent No More' they've proved it can be learnt, bought, transferred, inherited or stored. But wisdom cannot be gained by any of these methods, only God gives wisdom.

I am not even going to talk of the pride of those without proper worldly knowledge. Those that shunned and continue to shun every form of education, especially the sound truth of the bible but are puffed up nevertheless because they snack on regurgitated information passed down from ill-informed and biased sources especially the media. In most cases it is not even second hand knowledge but fifth and sixth hand and in their case, the old adage is true and consistent; 'empty vessels make the most noise'.

But both groups don't even compare to this third group I am about to describe. They have some grasp of worldly knowledge because they have forged friendship with those that do, either by way of partial education (Didn't finish the course), employment or property in the right area and converse with the right accent and tone. They are worse because they have neither spiritual nor natural substance but are more puffed up than the other two and are in denial about their position. Oh and they feel they are better than those of the second category. These people are the poorest of all.

Despite this, it is a great folly because those with worldly knowledge, the ones that pretend and those without lack true wisdom. We all fail to see if what we have received lines up with the word of God and do not have the decency to ask Him if this is what He expects from His children and creation. No one questions or speaks out. Everyone cowers under the weight of tolerance with the powers of discernment completely desensitised by popular culture. For instance we endorse perversion and call it alternative lifestyle or families that fail to discipline their children and call it building self-esteem. What a joke! The parents themselves don't have any, so how can they build self esteem. No, they think self esteem is a jovial personality or wearing revealing clothes. Shocking!"

"You do 'half' make long speeches but you're spot on again. No one can tell what is good or bad behaviour anymore, and even if they can, they refuse to speak out or act. Staying on the fence because they think they are not directly affected, well I have news for you, it affects all. For example, every child that is hungry, homeless, abused, deprived or discriminated against is everybody's responsibility. I said passionately."

"Ellis. It says wisdom is the principle thing. Jesus Christ is wisdom. He is the wisdom of God. He has the key to unlock all knowledge and give understanding in how to use knowledge effectively. What I am saying is that, His wisdom will give you a passion to see others flourish, turning your selfish and miniscule knowledge into a spout of health to you and others."

"I agree and........"

"Hang on a sec;" Idika interrupted. "Let me get my pocket Bible out. Here read Proverbs 8 you'll see how wisdom (Jesus) stands in the street corners crying out loud to all mankind to gain prudence and understanding."

He handed it over and I started reading:

Does not wisdom call out?
Does not understanding raise her voice?

On the heights along the way
Where the paths meet, she takes her stand

To you, O men, I call out
I raise my voice to all mankind

You who are simple, gain prudence
You who are foolish, gain understanding.

Listen, for I have worthy things to say;
I open my lips to speak what is right

My mouth speaks what is true
For my lips detest wickedness.

All the words of my mouth are just
None of them is crooked or perverse

To the discerning all of them are right
They are faultless to those who have knowledge

Choose my instruction instead of silver
Knowledge rather than choice gold

For wisdom is more precious than rubies
And nothing you desire can compare with her

I, wisdom, dwell together with prudence
I possess knowledge and discretion

To fear the LORD is to hate evil
I hate pride and arrogance
Evil behaviour and perverse speech

Counsel and sound judgement are mine
I have understanding and power

By me kings reign
And rulers make laws that are just

By me princes govern
And all nobles who rule on earth

I love those who love me
And those who seek me find me

With me are riches and honour
Enduring wealth and prosperity

My fruit is better than fine gold
What I yield surpasses choice silver

I walk in the way of righteousness
Along the paths of justice

Bestowing wealth on those who love me
And making their treasuries full

The LORD brought me forth as the first of his works
Before his deeds of old

I was appointed from eternity
From beginning, before the world began

When there were no oceans, I was given birth
When there were no springs abounding with water

Before the mountains were settled in place
Before the hills, I was given birth

Before he made the earth or its fields
Or any of the dust of the world

I was there when he set the heavens in place
When he marked out the horizon on the face of the deep

When he established the clouds above
And fixed securely the fountains of the deep

When he gave the sea its boundary
So the waters would not overstep his command
And when he marked out the foundations of the earth

Then I was the craftsman at his side
I was filled with delight day after day
Rejoicing always in his presence

Rejoicing in his whole world
And delighting in mankind

Now then, my sons listen to me
Blessed are those who keep my ways

Listen to my instruction and be wise
Do not ignore it

Blessed is the man who listens to me
Watching daily at my doors
Waiting at my doorway

For whoever find me finds life
And receives favour from the LORD

But whoever fails to find me harms himself
All who hate me love death.

(NIV)

The minute I finished reading it, the words that came out of my mouth was; "praise Jesus. Men, I need to really meditate on these words. The fear of the Lord is the beginning of wisdom and understanding is to shun evil. I feel that society...."

"Sorry mate, indulge me for a moment, let me just make this point." Idika interrupted again and continued.

"The people in the so called upper echelons of society are just as decrepit as those that lack education or the prescribed etiquette of society. The only difference with the upper crust is that theirs is coated and masked by there luxurious surroundings, hand made sequined garments and stomachs that belch out champagne, caviar and canapés after an evening at Chateau Ossie Nwamama. But 'all flesh is like grass and all its glory like the flower of grass. The grass withers and the flower falls but the word of the Lord abides forever. That word is the good news which was preached to you'."

Smiling I said, "The upper crust you just portrayed describes the ideals every music video tries to sell to society."

"Well, they are part of the deluded concept of high society. New money however it is made challenges the stereotypes of who belongs in the upper crust and rightly so." Idika said and continued;

Back to Love!

"But in all seriousness, back to my point on God being the foundation of true enlightenment! You and I at diverse times have not shown love. I thought I knew and expressed love but I was so off the mark, it was unbelievable. But I am now walking in the corridors of elucidation and illumination and it is now expressed properly because I walk in His word. So instead of just reading about the qualities of love in Corinthians 13, I ask The Holy Spirit to help and guide me in putting them into practise."

"I know what you mean. The whole Bible is God's love letter to mankind. You cannot effectively love without loving God who is love, knowing His love and experiencing His love. The cross stands as God's ultimate love sacrifice for the world. All we have to do is receive that love.

I mean love is not just about the affections we show to each other but a condition of the will. Hence some people feel love is gone once the emotional high disappears and quickly conjure up romantic gestures to rekindle it. This is also why some people feel they have to have those turbulent relationships where there are constant ups and downs of the emotions or else their love is not alive." I said.

"You are right Ellis. I have heard some people say the best part of fighting with a spouse is making up, rightly so but don't do it just to be affirmed. These people only love with their emotions. They are easily stirred by all kinds of romantic gestures, especially fake ones. Some even see abusive relationships as love because they are hooked on the emotional highs and lows. Very sad!" He said.

"Yes very sad, people fail to realise that you have to purpose in your heart to love someone, not only because of how they make you feel but because you have purposed in your heart to show and express love. So that when the emotions you feel don't line up you can still love and be in that relationship. To truly love, every aspect of the senses must be operating equally, but the consent of the will must be the most functional."

"Ellis, the Greek language best describes love because it has three different types of love; Eros, Philos and Agape. This is crucial for understanding and clarification since parts of the Bible was written in Greek. Eros is a sensual love based on physical attraction, which we are all masters of and base our entire futures on. Philos is a love between friends and Agape is an unconditional love. Agape is what The Most High displayed on the cross and this is what He extends to us daily. It sees beyond our flaws, physical attributes, rebellion and assets. Also Agape is what He wants us to have and give. It is devoid of human emotions and certainly isn't utopian because Jesus Christ has demonstrated this love and if we learn of Him we will also. If only when we receive this unconditional love we are able to channel it to others without any dilution or prejudices our lives would be fuller and more rewarding."

"I hear what you are saying Idika. The love that we show to one another if it is not sprinkled with or coated in God's agape love, the actual reality of it, is harmful. It produces cancerous emotions such as obsession, possessiveness, hero worship, fear, dependency and depression to name but a few, in the giver and recipient of that love. Majority of the time the love we have and give regresses into these negative emotions because we are not actively seeking His love or letting His love guide our responses. Bruv, people inflict pain on their spouses, children, parents and friends while professing they love them deep down. In some extremes they even kill in the name of love and it shouldn't be so!"

"May God help us all," Idika said prayerfully. "God's love is crucial for humanity because it is consistent and holds all things together. His agape love that flows through Jesus Christ into our higher nature influences and renews our lower nature. This is essential because our lower nature is the possessor of all these negative emotions and God's love is what defeats it. So we need to constantly tap into the flow of His love and let it burn brightly within us. And just as Solomon observed; 'many waters cannot quench love, rivers cannot wash it away; if one were to give all the wealth of his house for love, it would be utterly scorned'."

Nodding I said, "So love is also a commitment of the will. And someone I can think of that learnt from the Master will be Dr Martin Luther King. He made love his stance all those years ago, because despite the adversity he faced in the pursuit of freedom for blacks in the U.S, his outlook was never racist. Instead, he championed the struggle of helpless people and conquered by standing on the wings of love and pitching his tent in its dynamic power."

Just before I finished talking Idika started walking but as opposed to the fast swerving sprint, we were gently gliding along.

Then he said; "you are absolutely spot on but do you know that the greatest battle that's ever taken place was motivated, orchestrated and accomplished by love?"

"Oh yes, 'greater love hath no man than this that a man should lay down his life for another'." I said

"Exactly, 'for God so loved the world, that he gave his only begotten son, that whosoever believes in him will not perish but have everlasting life'." Idika replied.

"Bruv, the purest form of love is revealed in Jesus Christ. He gave everything, I mean He gave!" I said the last bit quietly, half pondering the words I'd just uttered. (Just as the psalmist says 'Selah' which is interpreted as a pause or denoting a solo of a musical instrumental. Okay that aside, I suggest we use both interpretations at the same time. So let's pause for the soloist to play his or her stringed instrument and ponder what God Almighty gave and why you are running away from His love that beckons you to come. He won't force your will – it is your choice to claim your salvation that He has already purchased – will you do it? If so pray the simple prayer at the end).

"Yes He gave all," Idika's words drawing me out of my thoughts. "Love made Him come down to pave the way for a full reconciliation into a realm we had previously been banished from. So now we have a relationship with God the Father, God the Son and God the Holy Spirit."

To validate his point I showed him Ephesians 2: 14-18 from my own pocket Bible.

'But now in Christ Jesus you who once were far away have been brought near through the blood of Christ. For he himself is our peace, who has made the two one and has destroyed the barrier, the dividing wall of hostility, by abolishing in his flesh the law with its commandments and regulations. His purpose was to create in himself one new man out of the two, thus making peace, and in this one body to reconcile both of them to God through the cross by which he put to death their hostility. He came and preached peace to you who were far away and peace to those who were near. For through him we both have access to the Father by one Spirit'.

After reading Idika said, "Praise his Holy name."

Just then some teenager walked past us on platform 5 with his mobile phone blaring out Ludicrous and we caught the words; 'you move I move, just like that'.

I smiled and said "that's exactly what The Lord wants us to do, 'draw near to him and he'll draw near to you'."

And Idika said; "just like that!"

Trust!

"Oh and another thing I think you should highlight in your essay is trust." Idika added!

"Yeah, it is a key issue, because I think almost every woman I have gone out with in the past was very possessive, although my behaviour then warranted it but it was uncalled for. Besides, possessiveness stems from lack of self esteem."

Idika agreed and said; "it is a whole different bondage that needs to be destroyed because going out with that sort of person is like having an empty glass. You constantly have to fill it with words of affirmation and that will drain every ounce of emotional, mental and physical strength you have."

"It is even worse when you're not even doing what they're accusing you off, so you might as well do it." I said.

"Then their dysfunctional behaviour rubs off on you and before you know it, you are manifesting their possessive and jealous traits. The best thing is not to get involved with that sort of person or if you already are, seek the Lord and let His word guide you or you'll never have any peace." Idika said shaking his head.

I explained that "we are advised by The Lord to flee all appearance of evil and possessive and jealous people want you all to themselves 24/7 and that is evil. You'll never have peace or trust in that kind of relationship.

I mean, trust should be a function in relationships not an immutable quality that one person has and the other has to discover. Trust only grows when information is passed freely. Then it evolves into transparency and this should be the aim and watch word of every relationship.

"I agree"! Idika said and added. "Unlike love, trust has to be earned and the exchange of information and disclosure of character traits have to be on every level and applied to facilitate its growth in every relationship. Take work for instance, managers, team leaders and colleagues, horde information because they feel if they share, you'll know just as much as they do."

"Well they say knowledge is power, (the question is what kind of knowledge?) I said smiling, but I hear what you're saying."

Idika continued "companies that have people that horde information stifle the progress of the company or the ability to build trust. I think people fail to realise that a company is made up of people and the guy with the most mundane task plays just as important a role as the geezer that calls the shots."

I had to share with Idika what the Holy Spirit just impressed in my heart. "Just like when Paul talks about the body of Christ being made up of different members, each one playing a specific role. With the least and less visible members in the kingdom held in higher esteem than the visible and more 'glorified' ones."

"Didn't I tell you that Jesus had every aspect of life covered in His word? He had already put forth the principles and doctrine of "division of labour" even before Adam Smith thought of it." Idika said with a big smile.

"So no part of the body can function properly without the other parts being active and made aware of what is going on. Jesus is the head of the church, which is His mystical body and through the Holy Spirit, information is constantly passed to His members so we are not ignorant about the inheritance He purchased for us on the cross." I said.

"You are so 'on point' I could just shout for joy and 'you know the victory reside in the tents of the righteous of the Lord. For the Lord's right hand has done mighty things for us, His right hand reigns on high' – alleluia!" Idika said.

"Look mate, I continued. One of Dr King's quote that I like says; 'You can't be what you ought to be, until I am what I ought to be. And I can't be what I ought to be, until you are what you ought to be'. This should be the by-word for individuals, families, companies and society at large."

"Certain political parties will make you their leader with quotes like that." Idika said laughing.

"It is not a quote with any political leaning – it is steeped in the fact that all men are caught in an inescapable network of mutuality tied in a single garment of destiny. Whatever affects one directly, indirectly affects all. Also it is steeped in the desire to see other people rise to their station. And how helping them, will help you rise to yours. But the key as far as I am concerned, is aligning yourself with those that also want to see you get to your station not pull you down or stifle you. This is what families should live for and then extend it to society at large."

Idika smiled and said, "I agree. I don't think that anyone is better than I am and I don't think I am better than anyone – but I do recognise and appreciate that you have skills and gifts that I don't have. Instead of comparing and competing, I would rather we found ways to work together and use our different talents to improve our lives and in the process lighten and make someone else's existence more bearable."

I smiled and then said, "The Holy Spirit is an advocate of this saying. In His role as the administrator of the body of Christ, He is forever forming the mind of Christ in God's children. He imparts Jesus' life and binds each soul together through the ages. One of the ways He does this is by dispensing the necessary information to the departmental heads (5-fold ministry) and confirms it by giving it to the members for validation and authentication.

(This argument is inter-linked because there is a strong correlation between both).

Now, just like office companies and society in general, it is left for those who receive it to articulate and express it, without distortion or dilution of any kind. The aspect of receiving is the duty of all that hear. If you lack the ability to receive ask The Holy Spirit in Jesus' name. It is His task to help you in all aspects. Just as you'd ask whoever is in charge for help, although companies prefer those that require minimal assistance. But with the body of Christ, The Holy Spirit is patient to make sure you obtain, attain, retain and implement.

It says, you are 'blessed and made a blessing'. In other words, you are blessed when you receive and you have to give, so that you are a blessing to others. By this process, the Lord establishes His covenant with you. What you do with what you are given determines if more will be given to you. The productivity of companies hinges on how people share information and relate to each other and it also applies to families, because it builds trust.

Honest communication will indicate if a member is lacking in any aspect of their lives, so the others can rally round them positively. But it is imperative that each individual allow The Holy Spirit to put them in positions where they can receive His instructions."

"I hear what you are saying Ellis", Idika said. "And I thank God for giving me a family that strive constantly for transparent and honest communication. It is hard but due to this, our trust level is quite strong. But I am going to fall back on what we've stressed. To receive The Holy Spirit's instructions requires aligning yourself with Him. And the only way to do this is to make Jesus Christ your Lord and Saviour – period."

"Exactly" I said! "He made us unique and has special information that pertains to us, but some people go through life never realising or knowing their particular contribution or why they are unique."

Idika nodded his head and said; "our relationship with Him blesses us, our family, nation and the world at large. He said to Abraham, 'I'll bless you and in you will all nations be blessed'. God wants us to impact the earth. Why, because we are; 'the seed of Abraham through Christ Jesus'."

With less hand gestures, I said, "So the Holy Spirit is forever nourishing and empowering the body of Christ with information about all the Father has given to our Lord Jesus. Also helping us, communicate to the Father through Jesus."

Idika's smile broadened as I continued.

"Trust is built on the free flow of communication. This process has to be translated in all 'our various' types of relationships. Employers need to communicate and share information freely with employees and vice versa. Husbands need to communicate with their wives and vice versa. Parents with their children, friends with friends and this sort of communication should be truthful and done not only when it is convenient but always. And for trust to truly flourish you have to listen and take on board what is said, not your pre-conceived notion."

"Yeah, that's one of my biggest problem areas. I think I listen but not as attentively as I should." Idika said, displaying that honest trait again.

"Look, listening is the most important part of communication, especially when it is done without prejudice or assumptions. That way, you would be able to discern aural messages without any of these undue barriers. I mean, in a world where everyone is trying to out talk the others, the person that listens and understands is king. Funny, in this age of varied and diverse communicative tools that can have the entire world talking in seconds, the cry of every human being is still 'no one is listening to me', shocking!"

"Okay, so lack of transparency and accountability is vital. How about governments?" Idika asked.

"And governments too, they certainly don't listen. They also suffer from a split personality. They talk the talk but certainly don't walk the walk. Total lack of congruence if you ask me!" I replied.

"Oh, don't forget mild amnesia on top of their split personality! Only one word encapsulates the characteristics of government: rhetoric." Idika said laughing.

Very dry humour if any but I was laughing also. Then I said. "Seriously this lack of communication, transparency and accountability has hindered the progress of whole continents. Governments need to foster relationships with its citizens. This is vital for national progress and global unity. The whole exercise of communication is to listen, take on board and respect the wishes of the electorate. (This is why dictatorial regimes must cease to exist and hopefully without bloodshed) I feel voters should bear a grudge if these aspects are not practised and express it at every given opportunity. Hopefully, the elected will be reminded of their position, who put them there and what their basic function is – to represent the people."

"It's like, how they all continue to disappoint families, failing to understand and recognise that unless rights have meaning at home they have no meaning anywhere else." Idika said!

"Yeah, they think they can legislate morality." I said with finality.

Betrayal!

When the train to Syon Lane pulled up we got on and sat opposite each other next to the window. The minute we were seated Idika changed the direction of the conversation but stayed with the theme.

"As with everything, it takes time to build and establish a trusting relationship, but it only takes one incident to bring it all crashing down. Our relationship with the Lord is based on trust. He says; 'trust in the Lord with all your heart and lean not on your own understanding; in all your ways acknowledge him and he will make your paths straight'.

Once we are saved, The Holy Spirit gently shows us how to enter His presence, by reading the word, meditating on the word, praying and just worshipping Him. We in turn have to now remember the road map of this reverential relationship, by cultivating His presence through constant praise and worship, walking in obedience and letting His word renew our minds. And each day 'like' clock work His mercy wakes us up and the trust level increases, as we yield and submit to Him."

"Yep, just as we cultivate our everyday relationship," I said.

"Exactly! I'll give you two guesses, what are the two most dangerous weapons to a relationship?" Idika asked.

"Hmmmm, lack of communication!" I answered

"Yes", Idika said and asked. "And?"

"I can't think of another," I shrugged.

"Infidelity," Idika said like a cat with the milk. And then he continued:

"Lack of communication is dangerous as it affects all forms of relationships. Even on a football pitch communication is important because it doesn't only build trust but also understanding. That interaction on and off the pitch might then become telepathic because you've now moved from just verbal, to using the whole anatomy to express what you have to say. Just like Andy Cole and Dwight Yorke. All Cole had to do was watch and anticipate which shoulder Yorke would drop to know what run to make behind the defenders. The understanding was so transparent that Cole could predict what to do from the different types of smiles on Yorke's face – although he never stopped smiling.

Communication transcends just verbal utterances, as we all know and all must be used to foster and maintain a trusting relationship. But the basic form of communicating is verbal and must be used above all because people can't read your mind and very few understand body language. So you have to let them know how you feel and what you want. They in turn should respect your feelings and this can only be achieved if the other important aspect of communication is active; listening. Just as we've stressed, people need to learn to listen.

But Infidelity! Men, just the thought or the mere mention of it, releases venomous darts, that are so deadly that only an antiserum of dinner, flowers, chocolates and a constant reassurance of undying love will seal the crack. The poison it secrets is suspicion and the incubation period is faster than an f14 fighter jet. Also suspicion is close relatives to insecurity, low self esteem, jealousy and revenge. Revenge is the last of the relatives but it is eagerly waiting to act, just in case the crack is not mended quickly enough for suspicion to develop into pain."

So I said; "I am sure the people that have already manifested traits of suspicion and it's relatives, the incubation process is zilch, because in those people these characters don't just get invited once the poison is released they are already living there. In fact they had spent the previous night whispering to them that their partner lied about their train being delayed."

Idika laughed and said "you are very funny."

"No, but it's true, I don't even want to talk about jealousy because where there is jealousy there is envy, strife and every other kind of evil. These relatives need to be dealt with from the root. I've seen them in office buildings, train stations, street corners, bars, churches, and in the past I have dated and even shared a home with them. But never again, so thank God."

Still laughing, Idika added, "this is why our vertical relationship has to be established and centred on Jesus, because then our horizontal ones will be fruitful in every sense of the word. There is nothing as effective at building trust like transparency and if you are transparent you'll certainly endeavour to be honest.

Ellis, God hates infidelity and is cross when His children worship other gods. We in the Western world might not necessarily have wood carved images or shrines that we bow to, but we are constantly bowing at a different alter. We have substituted those old fashioned idols for new ones and now worship people, money, careers, houses, cars, various sports and Hollywood. There is nothing wrong with having things or dreams but don't let them have you. If you place your emphasis on things thinking they'll satisfy you, you'll be forever chasing and searching without ever getting true contentment. Only God can fill that void and provide true satisfaction."

"Yeah, we have to be focused on Him and then He'll give us the ability to truly enjoy and appreciate these perishable things." I said.

Idika nodded in agreement and said, "He has to be number one in our lives and because God despises infidelity, so does every human being. It is one of the most destructive weapons and quickly brings down whatever trust that's been built up. His perspective on it is this:

'if you are married your body is not yours but that of your spouse', so why are you using it to do what your spouse will not consent to?"

"I am sure most women will want their men to hear this, especially those that behave like dogs." I said smiling.

"Perhaps but they are just as active as men when it comes to infidelity, the difference is that women are more subtle in their ways and use more discretion. But since society no longer frowns at any behaviour of promiscuity or adulterous liaisons it's as if women have just started doing it. Granted, men have a disposition that is harder to control and easily excitable but women do too, especially when they are not properly loved. Nevertheless both sexes are equally culpable and likely to be unfaithful.

If you truly love and honour that special person in your life you'll realise that you stand to lose almost all by that action, whether you get caught or not. It will totally shatter the trust and the rebuilding process is twice as hard.

But if we have the fear of the Lord and know we are accountable to Him, we'll also thrive to be accountable to those we hold dear in our lives. And the fear of The Lord is not just the beginning of wisdom but also a natural repellent for all the lethal weapons that try to break our relationships.

The enemy is constantly poised to attack every stride we make towards building a trusting relationship with God and man. But glory to God that Jesus has all power and greater is He that's in us than he that's in the world."

"Oh yes", I said in the tone of that dog from the Churchill car insurance adverts. "So we move forward with confidence knowing He has made us over-comers through Jesus Christ."

"Yes sir!" Idika said.

Success!

I was framing my essay mentally when I remembered an important point, so I said, "how about unforgiveness?"

"Now that's like catching a piranha with your bare hands and taking it home." Idika said. "Again, let me just give you the Lord's perspective on this and let it guide you. He said and I am paraphrasing here. Before you bring your gifts make sure you've made peace with your brother or neighbour. I mean He told Peter roughly how many times we should forgive, 70 x 7. And Dr King explained it best, when he stressed that this teaching does not hinge on the amount of times you forgive, before you start doing the maths and only forgive 490 times. But God is about conforming us to the image of His Son. So by the time you've forgiven to that amount, forgiveness will then be part of your character."

"You are absolutely right because if we regard unforgiveness in our hearts He won't hear us when we pray." I said solemnly.

"Hmm," Idika said. After a pause as if to gather his thoughts he said, "it's a case of going to Him in prayer and asking for the power to forgive and to forget. Otherwise, it will develop and fester into pain. Unforgiveness is the cholesterol that clogs the spiritual arteries and produces fruits such as stress, skin damage, emotional and mental trauma and physical sickness. It's very cancerous and besides not one human being is worth losing God's presence."

Smiling I said, "Therapist eat your heart out."

"Ellis, trust me, His word is the foundation of everything and faith is simply, believing everything He says. The reason we don't is because we don't know Him. Our fallen nature is entrenched in and has greater faith in doubt and unbelief. But once we know Him, we'll see that He never changes and is always faithful and loved us while we were yet sinners. If we have this mind, faith in Him will grow and develop for it works by love. And love demands intimacy!

Check this out, in Isaiah 55, He said; 'Everyone that thirst, come ye to the waters and he that hath no money; come, buy wine and milk without money and without price. Wherefore do ye spend money for that which is not bread? And your labour for that which satisfies not? Hearken diligently unto me, and eat ye that which is good and let your soul delight itself in fatness'.

We only know how to feed our flesh and lust but He alone knows how to feed and truly enrich our soul. In Him I am truly satisfied and He is the most joyful sustenance for my being."

"Yeah that's cold! The Lord is marvellous beyond comprehension." I replied. (Oh, almost forgot, street lingo again. 'cold' means 'bad' sorry it means brilliant, good, awesome, fantastic. In fact all the good superlatives you can come up with that you think can be accorded to the Most High.) (Lord thank you that in your divine mercy you even allow our unworthy words such as marvellous to praise your holy name. We've made words such as marvellous unworthy through frivolous use. Actually one of the names of Jesus is Marvellous Counsellor).

"Em, Ellis one more thing you can throw into your piece would be self disclosure. People constantly lie to themselves. I mean how can you build a trusting relationship if you can't tell yourself the truth?"

"You are right," I agreed with Idika. "We can never be truly successful if we don't tell ourselves the truth."

"It sounds ridiculous to even contemplate that people lie to themselves, doesn't it?" Idika asked.

I answered, "Of course if does. Some people distort and lie to themselves about how they got into a certain predicament and choose to blame others. When they know full well that no one is responsible for where they are but themselves. This blame culture is so bad that no one takes responsibility for their actions."

"Perhaps their meaning of success only relates to careers and financial prosperity." Idika added.

"I think you've just mentioned another key point. How can you be successful if your basic relationship is the 'pits'?" I said to Idika

"Yep, those types of people only foster relationships from a selfish base – what's in it for me. Their main tool for building relationships is manipulation and you don't even want to mention extremes people like that, go to, to get their own way."

"Funny I was reading a book by Charles Swindoll a couple of weeks ago and he expounded on Emerson's take on success. I am not sure if you're familiar with Swindoll or Emerson?"

"I respect both a lot." Idika said smiling.

"This is how he measured success:

To laugh often and much
To win the respect of intelligent people & the affection of children
To earn the appreciation of honest critics and endure betrayal of false friends
To appreciate beauty
To find the best in others
To know even one other life has breathed because you live

I think I must have missed out one, oh well what Charles was saying was that Emerson never once referred to rank, status, money, fame or power. Neither did he mention size or statistics. Instead we are asked to pay close attention to the verbs to laugh, to win, to earn, to endure, to appreciate, to find and to know."

"Wow, I have to get hold of that book – strong stuff," Idika said.

"Basically" I continued. "The emphasis on how to be successful is placed outside of our self and strictly falls on how we treat others."

"Exactly, after all, Jesus said if we do unto one of these (people in need) we would have done it unto him. Men, our motive and thoughts play an important role in what we produce. Idika said happily and I think he was delighted because he just learnt something new.

Then I quoted what Jesus said, 'out of the fullness of the heart the mouth speaks' and 'as a man thinks so is he'. "So we need to forget those victim stories of constantly complaining or blaming others. Instead ask, how did I create that? What did I say or not say? And what do I need to do differently to get the results I want.

I can hear it now! All the words of advise from parents and friends; 'those girls will ruin you, stay away from that boy, go to school, get a job, stop being lazy, you can't sleep all day, your choice of friends add nothing to your life, drugs are not good for you, read your Bible and do what it says, we are only friends, I don't love you, I don't care if you don't love me in that way'. Men, the list is endless but when you reap the fruits of not heeding positive instructions you blame others by absolving yourself of your responsibility in the causation of your circumstance.

I know it is hard to go against the grain, especially when the enemy and your rebellious nature have conspired to make sure you do the very things that won't please God or your family (that's if you have family that know the truth of God's word). This why you have to hook up with the Lord to help you produce outcomes that will glorify Him, bring joy to your family and prosperity to your soul."

Just then my mind flashed back to the script and how imperative it is to be saying your lines from the right script – His script.

Idika buttressed my point by saying, “I am glad I hooked up with Jesus Christ. Check out what Dr Charles Stanley said; ‘success is Godly mothers raising Godly children in an evil world’.”

“Yep, I thank God for my mother’s prayers they certainly kept me in the loop. You know that what we’ve just talked about has been spoken of countless times and most people know this stuff but the problem is still rampant and rife in society.” I said.

“That’s why we have to keep talking about it and bringing it to the fore. We have to inoculate this generation and especially the future ones. It was Karl Marx who said; ‘a people without a heritage are easily persuaded’. This generation have forgotten the legacy left by God’s heavyweights such as John and Charles Wesley, Charles Spurgeon, Smith Wigglesworth, John Rainsford, William J Seymour, E.V Hill and David Watson, to name but a few. These men knew and walked with the Master.

I don’t know about you and I think I have said this before, but when I tried to execute most of the things we’ve just talked about, I failed miserably. I was relying on my own strength, but the moment I surrendered, He brought me out, cleaned me up and taught me how to live a life that’s acceptable to Him and those around me.” Idika said softly.

“I hear you bro,” I said. “Thank you Jesus is all we can say.”

Hippity Hoppity!

Then he said. “A while back I stumbled on some tune by Killah Priest a Wu-Tang aficionado, relevant and apt lyrics to what I was going through. I committed it to memory. It goes something like this. I can’t rap, so I’ll just say it:

My life, though things may seem hard
I know I can depend on God

So many types of women
The life that I was living
The clubs, the thugs, the nights
That I would give in.

It didn't feel right in my system
But I was with them
Trying to fight this feeling
But I was just like a victim

Caught up in the rhythm of dough
I was spending
Drinking down venom
The Bacardi and lemon
The bartender grinning
The party just beginning

I mean the stars, cars
The cards that you charge
To the broads that you meet at the bar
Is all a mirage

I even ignored my true calling from God
Hid like Jonah, in the club
With bottles of Coroner
Surrounded by models and owners
Cronic smokers, the ones that you find
In a coma, play the corners.

But today I'm no longer there
I am much stronger
Witness my words.

Take a straight shot of liquor
Leave a spot on my liver
Because the life that I got
Is nothing to live for!

My son is one and probably
Will survive hell

The Lord knows when
I searched, I needed therapy
My heart is beating heavily
Am seeking heavenly
For the rest of me

My men says stay weeded
That's the recipe
But the cops might arrest me

My destiny is to leave a legacy
I don't have much but if the Lord credit me
You'll see the best of me

I found a new life today
Within the Bible page
While the pop corn is in the microwave
I hop on a tidal wave
Of being stress free
I could do it if you let me
If I am wrong then correct me

My life, though things may seem hard
I know I can depend on God."

"I am totally feeling that," I said. I thought to myself how funny I've been able to build a relationship of trust with

Idika that he is spitting rhymes or rather reciting rhymes, since he lacked flow.

“I didn’t know you were a wordsmith?” I joked with him.

“What!” He said to me challengingly. “It was Billy Collins who said; ‘The urge to tie a poem to a chair with a rope and torture a confession out of it, lessens when poetry arises freshly each day’.”

“Whoa! The man knows his stuff,” I quipped. “Alright Tupac, check this out:

I’ll perspire to acquire
What I require
I won’t retire
But will re-fire!

What! What are you laughing about? It rhymes! Okay, okay check this:

My eyes are like photography lens
As I push pens
Only to serve my virtuosity
Unleashing a glittering salvo of words
My incandescent poetry
Lighting up the sky
Claiming to be the most potent
Wordsmith without a bank balance
Striking fear with my poetic sentence.”

“Yes mate”, Idika said moving his head from side to side. Just then the train pulled into Syon Lane station. Then he said, “Bad boy rhymes, all we need now is some b-line, a Rottweiler and loads of mates in hooded tops giving it large! Have to hurry to work though as I'd rather have my bank balance strike fear than my word play. I'll catch up with you later or tomorrow. Peace-out!"

Just like that he switched into turbo and zoomed off. I spent the rest of my journey into work trying to remember all the constructive points he made concerning my essay. I can't believe I didn't make friends with him at College – oh well. Precious Holy Spirit, I pray you help me remember all the vital points we made. I bless, praise and adore You.

Tête-à-tête!

Just then a friend from work, called Richard, strolled alongside me and said jokingly, "you look cute today."

I immediately retorted "no sale 'Miles Bimpleton', I don't ride that bike. Look Richard I'll take it you meant cool?"

"Come on, you know I am only winding you up." He replied.

"Yeah, yeah!" I said.

"So are you ready for me to teach you how to bring in the cheese, you know I'm the big cheese." Richard said.

"Yeah, you are the big Edam, the real mo cheese." I replied.

"Oh yes, I constantly bring in the stilton, with all my farm and cottage clients." Richard said with a smile.

"You are the dairy king alright," I chuckled.

The minute we got to work I jotted down most of what I could remember from my conversation with Idika. Throughout that day, my heart was just lifted up in praise to The Most High. I take breaks as often as I can to pray, and I took more than usual that day. His presence is always with me but I love it when we are alone, so I can lift up holy hands to Him in praise. He just showers and envelops me in it and I love nothing more than to just bask in His awesome presence.

That evening Richard and I left work at 5.10 in order to catch the 5.21 to Clapham Junction, just as we got to the Syon Lane station Idika turned up with a pregnant lady he introduced as a colleague.

After the pleasantries of introducing Richard to Idika and Brenda, then Idika introduced Brenda to me and Richard, I pulled him aside and said:

“Mate, did you get her pregnant at lunch time?” I burst out laughing.

“Very funny, the cheek of it,” he said smiling.

We rejoined the others laughing and I am sure they must have felt uncomfortable, oh well! I almost forgot Richard falls into the category of one of ‘these people’ that see the platform and train station as a way to ensnare a mate. He is always on high alert, trying to clock (street lingo, it means: look) and engage every skirt with his eyes and mannerism. Oh you might also be wondering what Richard looks like so I’ll give you a brief description.

Richard is your typical uber-latte drinking professional – must be seen with coffee in hand. He is about six feet, short dark hair, podgy stomach but a very friendly face and he is very friendly. Basically a harmless guy, that likes to get on with life without any conflict. Oh and he walks slower than a snail with both feet facing the opposite direction when he walks – very strange!

"So how far gone are you?" I asked Brenda.

"7 Months" she answered rubbing her stomach. It must be a natural instinct, because I've seen so many women do it when they talk about their pregnancy.

Brenda and Idika started talking about work characters and something about pay discrimination, so Richard and I talked about his ability to bring in the cheddar.

Once the train pulled up, we politely let Brenda get on first. Richard and I have worked out the exact spot to stand on if you want to be in first class. He feels it's his right to travel first class being the big cheese and all, good thing we did. The first class carriage on the new trains, have a four seater with a table in the middle so we secured that for a nice squared table conversation.

Once we sat down Brenda started firing out these questions.

"So Ellis, are you married?" She asked.

"Nope!" I answered.

"I know Idika isn't, how about you Richard?" She continued.

"I'm on the look out but relationship first." Richard answered with a loud voice and I am sure it was done for the benefit of listening ears, since this is his favourite subject.

"Brenda you make it sound like not being married is a crime!" Idika said.

"No just asking," her smile expanded, "I have single friends that I might hook you guys up with. I am guessing you're all about Idika's age."

"Yep, 30, 31 and 32" I replied focusing on her features. Striking jaw line and visible high cheek bones despite her pregnancy. Her big nostrils are more pronounced because of her skin tone, she is mixed race. Also I think they're an indication of how nosey she is. There's intrigue, inquisitiveness and plain nosey. Trying to match-make someone you just met is nosey but some women love nothing better than to play cupid.

"Are your friends good looking," Richard asked unable to hide his delight!

"What does it matter," I interjected, "I've seen your taste."

"It's alright Brenda, I am happy the way I am and besides when I am ready, I am sure I can ask." Idika said.

"Yeah same here," I sided with Idika.

"Guys think about it, recommendation is better since it cuts out all that hassle," Richard disagreed.

“What hassle? What, of approaching a lady and chatting to her?” Idika asked confidently.

“Yes, it’s a hassle,” Richard replied.

“That’s because you complicate it with too much reasoning and judgement. Just think back to when you were young and how easy it was to strike up a conversation.” Idika replied.

“It was harder then, besides we get Brenda to big us up,” Richard said.

“Yes but you don’t need anymore big ups, you’re already the ‘mo cheese’,” I chipped in. “Besides I’ve experienced both sides and they turn out to be something else.”

Ignoring me, Richard asked again, “So are your friends good looking?”

“Drop dead gorgeous! My friends are good women with good jobs to match.” Brenda said with a tone of assurance.

“So what’s wrong with them?” I asked.

“You’re cheeky you are,” She said.

So I continued “are these friends the ones that you want to keep in your circle? I know married women don’t like single females all up in their mix, hanging around their husbands. Or is it single women that like hanging around married men? I get confused.” I said with a smile.

“Boy, the lady is pregnant and your bluntness is hazardous to your health.” Idika said with a smile.

"Funny enough," he continued trying to lighten things up and change the direction because Brenda's eyes dimmed just then and I think I saw her nostrils flare up a bit. With its size a blast would either blow me away or suck me in, depending on if she decides to inhale or exhale.

"I kept bumping into this woman most mornings and sometimes on my way back, she would smile and I would respond but that was that. We got talking and arranged to go out for a drink but I refused to commit to a day citing work schedule and all that jazz.

One day as we're on the train our conversation got beyond the pleasantries of bad weather and horrible trains. She got personal by asking all these questions. You know, the relevant ones like are you educated and what you do for a living. My answers pleased her and I am sure the ticks on her list of criteria must have been flying because the space between us got smaller and smaller. Then she asked the million dollar question, if I was single, to which I replied yes, trust me she would have hugged me there and then and smothered me with kisses, if I didn't say 'but'. So I told her I had two kids and saw them over the weekends. Her next question expressed all her disappointment and sudden resentment. She said in a slightly harsh tone; 'so how did you manage to work, do a post graduate course, look after two kids and stay sane'? Men, her disgust was so obvious I refrained from telling her what I have had to endure since youth, despite being born of royal bloodline spiritually and naturally and heir to a throne in both realms (all done so the suffering and glory of the Most High might be made manifest). Instead, I said, you do what you have to do.

She immediately did some mental back pedalling by saying 'I like kids' but I think she also realised that her first outburst had blown her chances. I never saw her again. She must have changed routes or something. Talk about changing your route to work because someone doesn't fit into your mental perception of who you think they are. Bizarre!"

"Her fantasy got shattered or she probably changed jobs," I said with a smile, remembering my rant about these people. This woman whom he just described fell into two categories. She uses the platform or trains to ensnare a mate and I am sure she probably exhibited qualities of those flirting ratleys to gain his attention. Or maybe, he falls into the category of that testosterone charged guy that walked up to that girl. Somehow I doubt that about Idika, I think the fear of The Lord in him, the lessons and pain would prevent him from behaving in that manner. Aaargh! I had to arrest my thoughts to hear Richard say.

"Typical! Women and their list! I am sure very soon a date will hinge on what cleanser or facial wash we use." Richard said with a hint of anger

"At least she knows what she wants." Brenda said, voicing her support for the sisterhood.

"Not really because after her outburst, she back-tracked and said she likes kids. Her pre-conceived notion had already taken her imagination to church and the wedding reception, even before I said hi. But I thank God it ended there." Idika said.

"That's what we do. We always look at the long term." Brenda said with less conviction.

"Fair enough" I said, "but at least get to know the person first before you plan it out. The shock and outburst meant she left no room for surprises and quickly voiced her compromise to keep her pre-conceived plan intact. These types just want you to come and fill a role in their cloud cuckoo existence. Your choices, needs and personality will be eroded because she has already created who you'll be. Dangerous! So Richard I didn't know you used facial wash and cleanser, what brand?" I asked laughing.

"Yeah but Idika scored nine out of ten on her list." Brenda said with a smile rather childishly.

"As flattering as that is, I'll pass. Everything about her oozed selfishness because when she was ticking her list, she'd have noticed that, I wasn't asking her any questions in return. Instead this was a partial two way conversation, because it was a question and answer session to satisfy and feed her imagination." Idika said.

"I worry about people that imagine or visualise without the right information or the consent and participation of the other person." I added.

"I know they are very dangerous because they act it out irrespective of your feelings," Idika said, "Some girl once told me that she heard a voice in her head that told her she would end up with me. It wouldn't have been a bad thing, if she had asked me if I had heard the same voice and if I wanted to end up with her. I certainly didn't hear the voice and had no incline of ending up with her. Another one was convinced we were an item just because we danced together and started spreading rumours about us. Shocker! Trust me people have to be careful of the delusions of the mind and living in the fantasy island of such delusions because before you know it they want to make it a reality. But the problem is that a fantasy can never become reality. Unseen reality creates seen reality, while unseen fantasy creates seen fantasy. And fantasy always leaves someone hurt and the person doing the fantasizing never gets their intended wish. Yes, you should fantasise but before you act it out, especially if it involves another person make sure they are aware of the parts that involve them so they can make a choice to participate or not."

"I agree," I said. "For some, the list is used as a tool to gauge more information, which is all well and good. While others use the answers from the list to feed their fantasy, even if the answers are contrary to what's in their heads. I am telling you guys, some ratleys you're telling them that you are not after a relationship but their deluded mind is making them hear only the word relationship."

"You're probably too nice to them and maybe because you are still sleeping with them" Brenda said and continued. "For us girls, that messes up our heads because it sends out mixed messages. But in saying that, if someone says it is casual, it means it's casual. For me if both words and actions don't correspond then; 'his got to go'. I deserve to be treated with love and respect. I have a friend who nothing in her relationship suggests that her so called boyfriend loves her. I mean, he cheats on her. No I can't call it cheating because she knows about it and he even tells her about all his other conquest. He never takes her out or buys her anything nice but she is still saying; 'I love him and that he loves me'. In fact he has told her on numerous occasions that they're just friends that happen to sleep together occasionally. Crazy stuff as this in itself is wrong! She is definitely deluded and living in some fantasy land thinking a dirty dog like that loves her, especially when his words and actions say the opposite! So tell me more about these desperate women you boys have been tangled with?" Brenda asked mischievously.

Before I could answer Richard chipped in. "Sometimes the list is ridiculous. I had some girl say to me that she'd have gone out with me if she could stand my friends. It's not as if she is going out with my friends and why should I cut off my friends for her!"

"Good thing you didn't even think of giving up your friends. Or did you?" I asked smiling.

"Of course I told her where to go." Richard said, flexing his shoulders

"Sounds like you came across one with the Yoko effect." Idika said.

"What's the Yoko effect?" Brenda asked perplexed.

"Yeah, what's the Yoko effect?" I asked, still smiling.

"You know the Beatles! No? Rumour has it that she caused the rift; she broke up the 'fab four', hence the phrase the Yoko effect." Idika said, surprised, we didn't know.

"Oh, there are thousands of them out there, especially the ones that break up friendships by sleeping with your friends." Richard said.

"Men behave in exactly the same way. In fact they are worse when it comes to sleeping with their friend's squeeze." I said, but Brenda gave me a smile that suggested I was just saying it to appease her.

Idika agreed, “Men are just as bad if not worse.”

“Brenda let me ask your advice” Richard said. “I like this girl at work, what do you think is the best way to approach her?”

“Tricky one – not! Just ask her out. Does she know you like her?” Brenda asked.

“Yes she does and I have asked her via email but she didn’t reply.” Richard answered.

“Oh well it means she is not interested.” Brenda said not realising that this was a sensitive issue for Richard.

“Maybe she is playing hard to get,” I said, “You know how women are.”

“What do you mean how women are,” Brenda’s nostrils flaring up again. I must watch my words around her or I might get a slap or maybe she is hungry, you know eating for two and all.

“If you’re really serious, why don’t you send her some flowers with a note saying something nice like; expressions are only reflections of the heart and asking her out for dinner is one of yours. I am sure that should do the trick.” Idika said.

“Smooth operator, I like it,” I agreed.

“Yeah but she might still say no”, Brenda said and continued addressing Idika. “You have a lyrical soul.”

“I don’t understand?” Idika asked, obviously intrigued.

Then she said. “It means you can love under the best and worst conditions.”

“Wow, praise God!” Idika said.

“Yeah but what happened to going to a bar, meeting a girl buy her couple of drinks and then back to her place - is romance dead?” Richard said rather annoyingly.

Just then the train pulled into Clapham Junction station and Idika said; “it’s that attitude and approach that’s strangling its very essence.”

“See you guys tomorrow.” Idika said.

“Yeah see you guys later” I said to Richard and Brenda. “Oh Brenda! I am sure before you get to Waterloo, you’ll school Richard on your lovely single friends. He might need them, if the office ratley fails.” I don’t think Brenda was amused.

“Peace-out Edam!” Richard said and Brenda smiled at Idika and mumbled a good bye to me.

Only by Grace!

“I don’t think she likes me,” I said to Idika as we strolled through the tunnel.

“It’s not that hard,” Idika said smiling. “She is cool though and Richard is a funny guy.”

“Yep, he is cool! So what’s that I heard about pay discrimination at work?” I asked.

"Bruv, you won't believe it, I found out recently that I am getting paid less than the other executives and we all do the same work. Basically when I moved to my new role, they said that I'll get a pay increase after 3 months. When the time came I didn't, so I asked but got excuses such as financial downturn. But what really stirred me was when I found out I was getting less than the others." Idika answered with a serious face.

"That's harsh! So what are you doing about it?" I asked again.

"I will go through the right channels and kick up as much storm as possible. I mean they knew I was getting paid less than the others and it never occurred to any of them to put it right even when I asked and complained. But it is also my fault for trusting that they had my best interest at heart." He said.

"That's cold! Your department must be tense?"

"It is and might get worse but I can handle it. Besides how can I run with the horses if the footmen weary me?" He replied.

As he said those words I thought to myself, he bears very little resemblance to a scholarly fellow, this is a warrior with words that are sharper than a two edged sword. My thoughts generated a smile that spread over my face and I said; He has made you a warrior and I'll pray for His grace to be lavished on you.

"Cheers," Idika replied.

When we got to our platform (15) it was packed with people. There was a delay of about 10 minutes on all services. “Typical,” I said but Idika didn’t answer, he was eaves dropping on the conversation by the couple in front us. From what he said to me I understood what they where talking about.

“Why do women ask, honey do you think I am fat?” What a question he said in a girlish voice. “I mean we can see that calorie laden adipose tissue and eager celluloid dimples through your clothes and you ask am I fat? You leave a guy with no choice but to lie. I am sure there are other ways to get rid of fat, instead of strangling it in clothes that are two sizes too small and cutting off the blood circulation.”

I laughed and said, “bro, you have issues but I hear you. I’ll catch the next train, because I’m going to Selhurst Park. Some friends invited me for dinner.”

“Cool, I am on my way to Shine, the unisex hairdressers on Streatham High Road, the Lord’s blessing.” He said.

“Peace-out” and I pushed my way onto the train when it pulled up.

I quickly sat down and brought out my pocket new testament bible. I normally read it on the train but hadn’t done so in ages. Although my intended book was Ephesians, I already had the pages of Romans chapter 10 folded, so I turned to it and noticed that I had verse 8 to 11 underlined. So I read it before going unto Ephesians.

The words of both books blessed me mightily that I have to share and as you are reading my diary, read on and let it bless you also!

Romans 10: 8-11
'But what does it say? The word is near you: it is in your mouth and in your heart, that is the word of faith we are proclaiming: That if you confess with your mouth, Jesus is Lord, and believe with your heart that God raised him from the dead, you will be saved, for it is with your heart that you believe and are justified and it is with your mouth that you confess and are saved.

As the scripture says anyone who trusts in Him will never be put to shame. For there is no difference between Jew and Gentile – the same Lord is Lord of all and richly blesses all who call on him, for everyone who calls on the name of the Lord will be saved'.

Then I flipped to

Ephesians 2: 1-10
'As for you, you were dead in your transgressions and sins, in which you used to live when you followed the ways of this world and of the ruler of the kingdom of the air, the spirit who is now at work in those who are disobedient. All of us also lived among them at one time, gratifying the cravings of our sinful nature and following its desires and thoughts. Like the rest, we were by nature objects of wrath.

But because of His great love for us, God, who is rich in mercy, made us alive with Christ even when we were dead in transgressions - it is by grace you have been saved. And God raised us up with Christ and seated us with Him in the heavenly realms in Christ Jesus in order that in the coming ages He might show the incomparable riches of His grace, expressed in His kindness to us in Christ Jesus.

For it is by grace you have been saved, through faith – and this is not from yourselves, it is a gift of God – not by works, so that no one can boast. For we are God's workmanship, created in Christ Jesus to do good works, which God prepared in advance for us to do'.

Before I got to the end of verse 10 my mind wondered to man's constant quest for all kinds of freedoms. Through the ages we have fought vehemently and passionately to win and safeguard various freedoms but we neglect the most important freedom of all; the saving of our soul. He wants us saved and because it is a free gift all we do is confess and accept the atoning work He did on the cross. There by aligning our self with Him and guaranteeing the most important freedom of all. The saving of our soul has a direct correlation and under girds our ability to walk in other freedoms such as prosperity and a sound mind.

Here is a revised definition of freedom. Freedom is not the ability or right to do what I want to do but the power to do what I should not do.

The Lord has made us free to choose and decide what we want, because if we are not able to do this, the Lord can't be ours. Free will is needful but to gain real freedom or enlightenment to understand the free will He has given us, we need Him. Unless we are taught by Him we can't truly be free human beings. Only by becoming His can we really 'be'. Our essence is only visible in His light. I'll say it again and it is said with tears, you can't be free with out accepting the atoning work of the cross. Westerners, we think that because our political system represents and stands for freedom that we are truly free. A guy in a despotic country that has Jesus as his Lord and Saviour has more freedom than a Westerner that just finished exercising his electoral rights by casting his vote. A poor housewife that has Jesus as her Lord and saviour has more happiness than a rich house wife that can't go to sleep without downing a bottle of vodka and consuming illegal amounts of sleeping tablets.

It is to freedom He has called us, come and walk in liberty. Come and be grafted in!

The Lord teaches that sense obeys reason and reason will bear sway to the senses. I am mine when sense serves and influences reason. But reason has nothing unless it is guided by The Lord. Reason on its own is pitiful and harmful but a right standing and perception of Jehovah intensifies His peace through the abundance of His grace and mercy. Besides, He is the Word and Reason of all reasons. So by having Jesus as Lord and always seeking Him and allowing His word to speak and guide me continually, then and only then can I be free and no longer a slave to sin.

Thank you Lord for your word in my heart and mouth!

The dinner at my friend's was good. I had my first organic potato and can already feel my toxins being sponged. Also I got to beat him at chess. So it was a good night.

Oh! And on my way back I bumped into Rob an old mate at Norwood Junction station, while waiting for my connection to Mitcham Junction. He wanted to swap old war stories about the killing field. But since he looked famished, malnourished and in need of sleep, I doubt he would make it back in one piece from his next tour. So I sensitively told him, how I had been air lifted and was only interested in peace talks, especially now that I am a representative of the Prince of Peace. So I explained how he can get air lifted into a place of rest. He adamantly insisted that I was missing out and called me weak. Gladly my train pulled into the station before he could tell me about the details of his most recent tour and his new crew members.

Funny someone else called me weak when I told them that I had re-dedicated my life to Jesus Christ. I totally agree with them and Nietzsche because I realised I have no strength on my own, but where I am weak, He is strong. Besides if you know someone that's willing and able to champion your course the wise thing to do is to let that person do it. Also this champion of mine has covenanted by legally binding Himself to take care of every aspect of my life and guarantees me victory through the assurance of His word, blood and life. And my part in this agreement is to kick back in obedience while acting by faith through love; thereby letting His grace and peace flood my heart. If gaining life is weak, then by God I am weak and endeavour to remain weak by trusting in His might, after all He has all power.

I confess it now and believe it in my heart, Heavenly father I am weak and if there is any aspect of my life where I am relying on my strength, please break my will and let only your will be done in my life in Jesus name - Amen.

After muttering this prayer and thanking God, my mind drifted to how easy it was to beat Dennis at Chess. Then I contemplated what I'd wear the next day. Seeing that it was Friday and dress down day at that. It's always better to dress down than to wear suits. Everyday suits just has 'rat race' stamped all over it. Maybe the khaki pants, the brown 'timbos', the black polo neck and the brown leather jacket. Yep, two matching colours and two strays that blend well with the other two. Yes sir, my sisters give good advice!

Men, because we've been emasculated, this is my plea to you. Seek the opinion of women when it comes to fashion. They blend colours better than we do. They have a whole section of their brain that's obsessed with beauty and looking good. Go on just ask, you know it makes sense. I once heard someone joke that when God created man, He looked at him, stopped and said I can do better than that, so He created woman. Get with the programme guys ask the ladies for tips, they are not called the better half for nothing.

The Future!

The following morning I was running a bit late but was able to catch the train. Idika happened to be on this train. This sort of co-incidence is becoming quite regular.

"Unlike you to be late," he said.

Idika was wearing blue jeans, faded green army T-shirt with the inscription 'the team works' white and blue Dada trainers and a blue double breasted jacket, but unbuttoned.

"I woke up late, but I had a strange night. I had three different dreams." I said.

"Heavy, but before you tell me about them read this, I copied it last night and I think it might help you with your essay. Sorry I keep coming up with all these ideas but the subject is close to my heart also. And since you enjoy poetry you'll understand what Yeats is saying". Idika said and then continued. "I got introduced to William B. Yeats at South Thames College by Rosie Persad and I've always enjoyed his work."

So I read:

Having inherited a vigorous mind
From my old fathers, I must nourish dreams
And leave a woman and a man behind
As vigorous of mind, and yet it seems
Life scarce can cast a fragrance on the wind
Scarce spread a glory to the morning beams
But the torn petals strew the garden plot;
And there's but common greenness after that

And what if my descendants lose the flower
Through natural declension of the soul
Through too much business with the passing hour
Through too much play, or marriage with a fool?
May this laborious stair and this stark tower
Become a roofless ruin that the owl
May build in the cracked masonry and cry
Her desolation to the desolate sky

The Primum Mobile that fashioned us
Has made the very owls in circles move;
And I, that count myself most prosperous,
Seeing that love and friendship are enough
For an old neighbour's friendship chose the house
And decked and altered it for a girl's love,
And know whatever flourish and decline
These stones remain their monument and mine.

"You don't need to torture a confession out of this poem, it speaks volumes. I have to get into Yeats. I like the bit about the vigorous mind, nourishing dreams and the warnings in the second stanza such as marriage to a fool, so as to avoid losing it." I said.

Idika nodded and said; "yes if families seek God, He'll nourish their dreams, especially those that glorify His name. If parents fight to pass on the dreams to their children, if they affirm and love their children, the tower will not be roofless.

There is something within man that screams out for rectitude, hence we have a conscience. But having a conscience is not enough, you simply can't break free without His help. The Greek word for man is Anthropos: meaning always looking up. Humans have something within them that wants to worship. This is why when we don't hear the gospel or know the Lord, we worship anything and anyone. This is the reason why so many live unfulfilled lives.

Ellis, Jesus is the key - The Most High that sits on the circle of earth is the key. We have to seek Him diligently and everything we've found in Him we have to proclaim to everyone. Then and only then, can we fight and save a lost generation from all kinds of physical, emotional and mental abuse. From drugs, alcohol, pornography, lust, promiscuity, self hatred, low self esteem, pride, poverty, diseases, religion and every other kind of bondage that I've missed out.

Jesus came to give us life and to give it abundantly. He is the fountain of life and wants us to bathe in the streams of His grace. Every human being has the potential to be conscious of their maker. I say potential because His salvation is a free gift all you have to do is accept it.

For you and me, our only duty on earth is to fear God and proclaim it. We have to tell them how our souls where land locked by the storms of pain, tortured by the whips of despair, chained by the cravings of the flesh and close to the pit of death but our Mediator was gracious and stepped in to spare us, because a ransom was found in Him. We have to tell them, how He restored our days and now when we pray we find favour with God and go wild with joy when we see His face because He has cloaked us with His righteousness. We have to tell them how we sinned and perverted what was right but did not get what we deserved, how He redeemed our soul from going down to the pit and now we will live to enjoy the light. God has done this thing, so His light will shine on us.

To tell them that, He is a father and wants the fatherless to experience His distilled and pure love that knows no bounds. He wants to put His arm around us, dry our tears and lead us through the spiritual and natural complexities of existence.

I've heard the cry of the fatherless in every street corner, ringing out daily. Their voices have gone out into the world!

Providence answered the cry when He paid the price on the cross and His resurrection is a confirmation that He triumphed and now has all power. We have to tell them because it doesn't matter what it is, He'll forgive. Jesus Christ is the answer!

He is the only father I've always known and because of that I am able to be a father to my kids. Ellis, He loves me with an eternal love and I love Him with all that I am, all that I have and all I'll ever be."

Idika's eyes were all watery. He didn't stop until we got to Clapham Junction and were seated on our train to Syon Lane.

"Sorry bruv, I had all that in me and had to get it out. So tell me about your dream?" He asked.

"Ok! It's cool, you're absolutely right. Jesus Christ is the key." I said and then I told him about my dream.

"The first dream, I was standing next to a bus, similar to the ones used by the National Express, but it was parked outside this shopping mall. Adults and kids were running by, joking and laughing, I heard a noise coming from a huge TV that was displayed in the shop window. Some one was preaching saying Jesus Christ, the Son of God is the answer but I couldn't make out the face of the preacher.

The second one, I was in a New York cab driving past a shop and again a TV and someone was preaching the same thing; Jesus Christ, the Son of God is the answer.

The third one, I was in this big auditorium with lots of people worshipping the Lord. This guy came on and started preaching that, Jesus Christ the Son of God is the answer. The person standing next to me said, tell him this is what he'll do and the message he'll preach. I turned around to see who said that but couldn't make out any face. I looked back on the platform to see who was preaching but again I couldn't make out the face but the frame looked familiar, then I woke up."

"Praise God and may His will be done in mine and your life." Idika said.

"Oh yeah Ellis, I forgot to tell you, I got an offer for my flat and an offer of a new job so I'll be leaving the juggernaut. I had asked the Lord in prayer and you know He answers prayers."

"Wow thank God, what a blessing and He'll continue to bless you. I am very happy for you bro. This is probably one of our last train rides then," I said feeling all emotional.

"Yep, but my gosh! You are highly favoured and blessed of The Lord. I pray that through your writings His name will be glorified and people will come to know Him."

"Amen to that," I said.

When we got off the train, Idika said peace-out and sprinted away in the other direction. Just then I knew why the Holy Spirit had led me to chat and become friends with him. Also at that instant, I knew he was the person preaching in my dream. They will want him now because life no longer haunts him. He has surrendered to a love that only sweet innocence brings. A love that is pure and simple!

God you move in mysterious ways but I thank you because you reveal it to your children.

Just then I recalled a note I had written to my best friend on the 27th Dec 2004:

Dear Holy Spirit

I have searched for consistency
In my life and character

I am totally convinced that man
Can never have one
Except he allows the Lord Jesus
To be his Lord and saviour

May the character of my Lord Jesus Christ
Always reflect and shine through
For here lies the consistency
In my life and character!

With those words floating in my head, I just praised and thank God for everything and especially these people I encounter everyday.

Ah! These people!

I watch you daily, taking notes of your demeanour and character to ascertain what your life is really like. I can't go by your dress sense, although sometimes I am so impressed that I bite your style and colour combos. I like it when you are full of beans with a happy countenance. Those times you strut around with the air of independence and confidence. Sprightly moving about because everything is falling into place and this is evident because you politely excuse and show courtesy to others. But I am more troubled when your countenance is sad. When the decisions and choices you are faced with weigh you down, when the external chug and internal strains of life are easily noticeable. Days when it seems the clouds and weather have conspired to go against you under the harsh influence of the moon and stars. Days when the emptiness of existence is what you know and the solitude and aloneness of your soul cannot be contained. Everyday as I make this journey as you do, I long to introduce you to my Father so that He can show you His love and heal you. Everyday I wish to share the peace and tranquillity my Father has given me with you, because He wants you to experience the same.

These people, I watch you daily and I am humbled that He chose me to tell you. And I know that you can choose to be chosen, since He has already chosen you...............!

The beginning of the End!

If like me you asked our Father for your inheritance and because of your petulant insistence He gave it to you without further remonstration – and you went into that far off country. The country where that evil prince rules – that place where you're being oppressed!

I have news for you! Our Father owns that far country and is standing at the gate eagerly waiting to see the silhouette of your shadow – poised for mobility. All you need to do is whisper I want to come home, Lord Jesus I need you and I am sorry. His grace and power is sufficient to free you the instant you whisper these words from your heart and bring you home.

By the way, we are waiting and ready to slaughter the fatted cow and throw the biggest party once you are home. We are all going to get down to the beats and sound of saints and angelic host; to the praise and glory of the Lamb of God who is to be praised forever more.

Come home – we miss you!! Call on His name now!!

Oh and you, yes you that have never acknowledged or made Jesus your Lord and Saviour. Call upon Him now – by simply saying the words below:

Lord Jesus I believe you are the Son of God. I believe you died on the cross and shed your blood for me. I believe you rose from the dead and ascended on high and that you are coming back to earth. Dear Jesus I am a sinner, forgive my sin, cleanse me with your precious blood and save my soul. Come into my heart. I give you my life. I receive you now as my Lord and Saviour. Fill me with your Holy Spirit. I am yours forever and will serve and follow you the rest of my days. Amen and Alleluia.

John 1.12 says 'But as many as received Him, to them He gave the power to become the sons of God, even to them who believe on His name'.

Oh lest I forget, the saints and angelic host will be raising the roof over your salvation. Party –time!

All you need to do is ask the Lord to direct you to a church where the word is taught, pray, read your bible and praise His Holy name. Kick back in obedience and act by faith through love and watch Him do above and beyond your expectations. Have faith in God!

Jesus is Lord!

Flip over for the shout-outs!

Dedicated to:

My children Luis and Bella, I love and cherish you. I constantly process and relive every moment I spend in your company and eagerly look forward with great anticipation and longing to your next visit. I am truly blessed to have you both in my life.

Hilda, I see it now. In you The Father didn't only give me a mother but also a mentor. I am grateful for your prayers, love, words of encouragement and honest criticism. You don't know how much I love you girl.

Okay, very few pages left and you are done.....go on flip over!

Notes:

"My Soul is satisfied" by Ed Kerr
Copyright 2000 Intergrity's Hosanna Music
Sovereign Music UK
Reproduced by permission
sovereignmusic@aol.com

Dr Martin Luther King Jr.
Reprinted by arrangement
Estates of Martin Luther King Jr.
c/o Writers House as agent for the proprietor
New York,
Copy right 1963 Martin Luther King Jr.
Copyright renewed 1991 Coretta Scott King.

Charles Swindoll's take on Emerson taken from:
Quest for Character by Charles Swindoll
Copyright 1982 by Charles R. Swindoll, Inc
Used by permission of The Zondervan Corporation

Karl Marx as quoted from page 46 of Rod Parsley's Book;
"Silent No More"
Silent No More by Rod Parsley
Published by Charisma House
Copyright 2005
Used by permission

Billy Collins, excerpt from "Introduction to Poetry"
From The Apple that Astonished Paris
Copyright 1988 by Billy Collins
Reprinted with the permission of the University of Arkansas Press
www.uapress.com

William Butler Yeats
My Descendants
Meditations in Time of Civil War
Used by permission A.P Watt ltd on behalf of Michael B Yeats

Vision of God
By Nicholas of Cusa
Copyright 1999
Used by permission The Book Tree

Killah Priest
My Life
Babygrande Records
Used by permission

Ralph Waldo Emerson
Nature 1836
Nature and Selected Essays
Edited by Larzer Ziff

Exercise secret: Constant!

The description of "Strange Woman" used in Inveigle relates to the Biblical view of a person with that spirit as described in Proverbs chapters 2, 3, 4, 5, 6, 7, 9: 13-18 & 23: 26-28

Bible quotes
Ecclesiastes 1:1
Ecclesiastes 7:26
Psalm 40:2
James 1:22
John 6:63
Isaiah 61:3

Hebrews 4: 15-16
Romans 1:16
Proverbs 22:6
Psalm 119:71
Psalm 139
1 John
Corinthians 13
Psalm 119
Philippians 3:10
Proverbs 8
Proverbs 4
John 3:16
Ephesians 2: 14-18
Psalm 118
Matthew 5:7
Matthew 22: 37-40
Isaiah 55:1-2
Romans 10: 8-1
Ephesians 2: 1-10

Unless otherwise indicated all scripture quotations are taken from King James Version of the Bible.

www.ingramcontent.com/pod-product-compliance
Ingram Content Group UK Ltd.
Pitfield, Milton Keynes, MK11 3LW, UK
UKHW021052270726
13967UKWH00012B/631